HAWK

Alpha Male Protector Romance and Suspense

A Guardian Hostage Rescue Specialists SHORT READ

ELLIE MASTERS

MASTER OF ROMANTIC SUSPENSE

JEM Publishing

Dedication

This book is dedicated to my one and only—my amazing and wonderful husband.

Without your care and support, my writing would not have made it this far.

You pushed me when I needed to be pushed.

You supported me when I felt discouraged.

You believed in me when I didn't believe in myself.

If it weren't for you, this book never would have come to life.

Also by Ellie Masters

The LIGHTER SIDE

Ellie Masters is the lighter side of the Jet & Ellie Masters writing duo! You will find Contemporary Romance, Military Romance, Romantic Suspense, Billionaire Romance, and Rock Star Romance in Ellie's Works.

YOU CAN FIND ELLIE'S BOOKS HERE:

ELLIEMASTERS.COM/BOOKS

Shop Ellie Masters Romantic Suspense and Steamy Contemporary Romance by series.

Angel Fire Rock Romance

Guardian HRS: Alpha Team

Guardian HRS: Bravo Team

Guardian HRS: Charlie Team

Guardian HRS: Delta Team

Cerberus Personal Security

The LaRouge Triplets

The One I Want Series

Angel's Peak Series

Billionaire Boy's Club

The Lovers

Changing Roles

SUGGESTED READING ORDER

Rescuing Angie

Rescuing Isabelle

Rescuing Carmen

Rescuing Rosalie

Rescuing Kaye

Cara's Protector

Rescuing Barbi

Charlie Team

Rescuing Rebel

Rescuing Stitch

Rescuing Mia

Jenna's Protector

Rescuing Sophia

Rescuing Malia

Rescuing Ally (Part 1)

Rescuing Ally (Part 2)

Delta Team

Rescuing Ember

Rescuing Aria

STANDALONES IN THE GUARDIAN HOSTAGE RESCUE SERIES YOU CAN READ ANYTIME

Military Romance
Guardian Personal Protection Specialists

Sybil's Protector

Lyra's Protector

Angel's Peak Series
Steamy Instalove Small Town

The One I Want Series

(Small Town, Military Heroes)

By Jet & Ellie Masters

The LaRouge Triplets

Brody

Cage

Billionaire Romance

Billionaire Boys Club

Hawke

Richard

Contemporary Romance

Cocky Captain

Romantic Suspense

EACH BOOK IS A STANDALONE NOVEL.

The Starling

The Swan

~AND~

Science Fiction

Ellie Masters writing as L.A. Warren

Vendel Rising: a Science Fiction Serialized Novel

If you enjoyed this book by Ellie Masters, the LIGHTER SIDE of the Jet & Ellie writing duo, and aren't afraid of edgier writing, you might enjoy reading BDSM themed books written by Jet, the DARKER SIDE of the Masters' Writing Team.

The DARKER SIDE

Jet Masters is the darker side of the Jet & Ellie writing duo!

Romantic Suspense

Changing Roles Series:

THIS SERIES MUST BE READ IN ORDER.

Command Me

Control Me

Collar Me

Embracing FATE

Seizing FATE

Accepting FATE

HOT READS

A STANDALONE NOVEL.

Down the Rabbit Hole

Light BDSM Romance

The Ties that Bind

EACH BOOK IN THIS SERIES CAN BE READ AS A STANDALONE AND IS ABOUT A DIFFERENT COUPLE WITH AN HEA.

Alexa

Penny

Michelle

Ivy

HOT READS

Becoming His Series

THIS SERIES MUST BE READ IN ORDER.

The Ballet

Learning to Breathe

Becoming His

Dark Captive Romance

A STANDALONE NOVEL.

She's MINE

To My Readers

This book is a work of fiction. It does not exist in the real world and should not be construed as reality. As in most romantic fiction, I've taken liberties. I've compressed the romance into a sliver of time. I've allowed these characters to develop strong bonds of trust over a matter of days.

This does not happen in real life where you, my amazing readers, live. Take more time in your romance and learn who you're giving a piece of your heart to. I urge you to move with caution. Always protect yourself.

Grab the First Book in The Guardian Hostage Rescue Specialists Series for Free

https://elliemasters.com/RescuingMelissa

ONE

Sawyer

THE MOUNTAIN DOESN'T CARE THAT I CAN'T SLEEP.

At 0200, the Guardian HRS training facility is a ghost town except for me and the automated systems that track my progress up this manufactured cliff face. My fingers find purchase on holds designed to test limits, and I'm three hundred feet up when my forearms start to burn—not from exertion, but from memory.

The scar tissue doesn't stretch the way normal skin does. Every reach, every grip, reminds me of melted helicopter metal and Tyler Brennan screaming while flames ate him alive.

"Morrison! Get me out! Get me—" Tyler's voice, raw with agony, still echoes in the worst dreams.

I can smell it even now—aviation fuel mixing with burning flesh, the acrid smoke that made my eyes stream as I gripped superheated metal with bare hands, skin blistering and peeling as I tried to bend what wouldn't bend.

His eyes through the cracked visor, wide with terror and trust—trust that I'd save him, that I'd be enough.

I wasn't.

The fuel tank exploded while my hands were still on the twisted frame, the concussive burst throwing me back, and when I came to, there was only silence and char where my buddy used to be.

The challenge coin around my neck swings free as I reach for the next hold. Tyler's unit coin, pulled from what was left of his flight suit after the fire died down enough to let me close enough to recover his body.

Two years, four months, sixteen days. The math runs constantly in my head, marking time since that Afghan mountainside became his grave.

The next hold is a crimper, enough for fingertips, but not much else. I have to dyno for it—a controlled explosion of movement that launches me upward. For a moment, I'm weightless, suspended between earth and sky, and the freedom of it almost makes me forget. Then my fingers lock onto the hold, tendons screaming, and I'm back in my body with all its scars and memories.

Three more moves to the crux—the hardest section where the wall goes past vertical into overhang. My core burns as I flag. My leg stretches out for balance, hooking a heel to maintain position.

This is what I come here for. The absolute focus required, the way everything else fades when it's just flesh and will against stone and rock.

My satellite phone vibrates against my ribs, the buzz traveling through my climbing harness. Only one person calls at this hour.

I rappel down fast enough that the rope heats through my gloves. My boots hit the ground in under a minute. CJ's name lights up the screen.

"Hawk." His voice carries the particular tension that means lives are on the line. "How fast can you get to San Francisco?"

I'm already moving toward the equipment room, stripping off my climbing gear. "What's the situation?"

"Emergency extraction. FBI analyst uncovered an imminent domestic terror attack—coordinated strikes in less than ninety-six hours. She tried to report it, and now her own agency is hunting her."

My shirt sticks to the sweat cooling on my back as I pull on tactical gear. "FBI doesn't eat their own without cause."

"Our CIA contact says she's got the only proof that can stop the attack. Someone inside wants her dead before she can share it." Papers shuffle on his end. "Savannah Cross, twenty-nine, Cybercrime Division. Photos on your phone."

I open the encrypted file while stepping into my tactical pants. Dark hair pulled back in a professional bun, hazel eyes that look directly into the camera rather than through it. Sharp intelligence in her face, something stubborn in the set of her jaw. Pretty in a way that makes me notice despite myself.

"What's her tactical background?"

"FBI analyst for five years. MIT graduate with dual degrees in computer science and mathematics. No field experience listed, but..." CJ pauses. "Her file's been sanitized. Someone deleted portions within the last seventy-two hours."

Interesting. Someone's trying to erase her before they erase her.

I strap on my shoulder holster, check the Glock 19's magazine, and chamber a round. "Location?"

"Apartment in Nob Hill. Address incoming. Hawk—" CJ's tone shifts. "Local FBI tried to bring her in six hours ago. Three agents went up. None came back down. SFPD is holding a perimeter, but they're being told to stand down by someone with federal pull."

Three dead agents changes the math.

This isn't a pickup—it's a recovery from hostile territory.

"Rules of engagement?"

"Get her out alive. Anyone trying to stop you is hostile." He pauses. "Guardian HRS will back whatever decisions you make in the field."

Translation: *Go weapons free preferred. Hot otherwise. We'll handle the cleanup.*

I grab my go-bag, already packed with medical supplies, extra magazines, and breach charges. "Pilot ready?"

"Ariel's spinning up now."

"Who else is joining me?"

"Flint took a bullet two weeks ago in Los Angeles, and Frost is still on medical leave. You're solo on this."

Solo's fine. Solo means I don't have to watch anyone else die on my watch.

The helicopter ride passes in mission prep—studying building schematics on my tablet, memorizing the neighborhood layout, and planning primary and contingency extraction routes.

Savannah Cross's apartment is on the eighth floor of a twelve-story building, with two stairwells, one main elevator, and one service elevator. Too many ways for hostiles to come at her, not enough ways to get her out clean.

San Francisco spreads below us in a carpet of lights and shadows. Ariel Black's voice crackles through my headset. "Two minutes to insertion point."

I clip onto the fast rope. "Put me on a nearby building, southeast corner. I'll make my approach."

"Copy. Southeast corner, coming up."

The skid touches down on a rooftop four buildings from the target. I drop into the darkness, and Ariel lifts away immediately. The night air carries fog and salt from the Bay, along with something else—the metallic scent of blood drifting from an open window.

I move across rooftops, using maintenance walkways and construction scaffolding to close the distance.

The fourth building has a fifteen-foot gap—too far to jump. I pull out my tactical grappling hook, the carbon fiber line whisper-quiet as it flies across the void. It catches on an HVAC unit, and I test it with two sharp tugs before committing my weight.

Hand over hand across the gap, San Francisco spread like broken glass and promises below me.

A couple argues in a nearby apartment below me, their voices carrying through an open window—normal life, oblivious to the violence about to erupt four buildings over.

The scaffolding on the next building is fresh, still smells of cut wood and industrial paint. Construction permits flutter in the wind, dated last week.

I use the exterior elevator shaft and climb the safety cage. My shoulder holster catches on a protruding bolt, and I have to contort to free myself without losing purchase.

Every second counts, but rushing means mistakes, and mistakes mean Savannah Cross dies.

The target building comes into view, and my instincts scream. Four black SUVs are arranged around the entrance, in the wrong position for standard FBI protocol.

The agents visible are wearing FBI windbreakers, but their weapons are wrong—MP7s instead of standard-issue MP5s. Their positioning is amateur, clustered instead of maintaining overlapping fields of fire.

I count twelve hostiles in total—four at the main entrance, two at the service entry, two more pretending to be homeless but with the telltale bulge of concealed weapons and tactical boots.

The rooftop has a sniper, poorly concealed behind an AC unit. His scope glints in the streetlight—rookie mistake.

These aren't FBI.

They're mercenaries playing dress-up, which means someone with deep pockets wants Savannah Cross dead badly enough to fund a private army.

I swing down to a seventh-floor balcony on the adjacent building, using my spotting scope to check Savannah's windows.

Curtains are drawn, but there's flickering light—muzzle flashes.

The pattern is wrong for a one-sided execution. Three-round bursts, then singles, then silence, then more fire from a different position. She's moving, fighting back.

The tactical part of my brain is impressed even as the human part knows she can't hold out much longer. The muzzle flashes are getting closer together—they're tightening the noose.

She's still alive. Still fighting.

I leap the six-foot gap between buildings, catching the maintenance ladder on the exterior wall. The metal groans but holds.

The seventh-floor window is locked—I use my tactical pen to shatter it at the corner, the sound masked by a passing truck.

Glass falls inward, and I follow, landing in a crouch in someone's hallway. A child's drawings line the walls—crayon superheroes and monsters, a normal family sleeping through a war zone. I move past their door, silent as smoke, taking the stairwell up one floor.

The eighth-floor hallway reeks of death—that particular copper-and-cordite cocktail that means close-quarters execution. The emergency lighting paints everything hellish red, turning blood pools black and making shadows dance like demons.

I climb fast, reach the eighth floor, and jimmy the hallway window. The smell of blood is stronger here, mixed with cordite and death.

The hallway is dark, with emergency lighting casting red shadows. Three bodies in FBI tactical gear sprawled near the stairwell door. Real FBI, based on their equipment.

Brass casings on the floor, but not from the FBI weapons. These are 9mm Parabellum, subsonic rounds designed for suppressed fire. Professional killers, not random thugs.

Someone orchestrated this to look like Savannah Cross killed three federal agents, adding cop-killer to whatever frame job they're building.

Each shot execution-style, close range, suppressed weapons. They never saw it coming.

I move past them, weapon up, following the sounds of combat from apartment 817.

Shell casings, every few feet, roll under my boots with tiny metallic clinking sounds. Someone's apartment door is cracked open, an eye visible in the gap before it slams shut—civilians smart enough to hide but curious enough to watch.

The sound from 817 is chaotic—furniture breaking, glass shattering, someone grunting in pain. Then a flash of white light under the door, followed by a man's scream. Whatever Savannah Cross is doing in there, she's not going down easy.

The door's been breached, hanging off its hinges. I slice the pie, taking the corner carefully, and the scene inside stops me for a heartbeat.

The apartment looks like a war zone. Furniture overturned to create defensive positions, kitchen drawers yanked out and emptied —she's been improvising weapons. Blood spatters the walls in arterial sprays, one body already down near the kitchen, clutching his throat where a knife found its mark. A laptop taped to her torso is visible through her torn blouse—creative and desperate in equal measure.

She's turned her home into a killing field, and she's still standing.

She moves like someone with training—not military, but something. Martial arts, maybe, the way she shifts her weight, always balanced, never over-committing.

When one of the fake agents rushes her position, she doesn't retreat. She redirects his momentum, uses his weight against him, and suddenly, he's stumbling into her knife range.

Savannah Cross wields kitchen knives like she knows how to use them. Her blouse is torn, showing the computer secured to her body. Blood—not hers—spatters her face. Aluminum foil balls litter the floor. Smart chick. She's made improvised flash-bangs from match heads and kitchen supplies.

Four men in FBI gear are trying to flank her position. She throws another foil ball, and it explodes in white light and smoke. One attacker stumbles back, and she puts a knife into his throat with disturbing accuracy.

Make that three.

The knife throw isn't lucky—she's practiced this. The rotation is perfect, the force exactly what's needed to penetrate the soft tissue of the throat. The man goes down gurgling, hands trying to stem the flow, but she's already moving, not watching her handiwork.

One hostile is advancing from her left, using the overturned couch as cover. Another is circling right, trying to get an angle through the kitchen. The third—the one I'm most worried about— is hanging back, speaking into a throat mic, probably calling in reinforcements.

They're coordinating, trying to time their assault.

Savannah doesn't wait for them to get set. She grabs what looks like a can of cooking spray and a lighter from beside her defensive position.

Homemade flamethrower.

The stream of fire forces the left-side attacker back, his FBI windbreaker catching fire. He drops and rolls, screaming, out of the fight temporarily.

But it's a feint. While they're focused on the flame, she's already moving, rolling right, coming up behind the kitchen attacker. He spins, raises his weapon, but she's inside his guard. An elbow to his solar plexus, a knee to his groin, and as he doubles over, she drives her knee up into his face.

The crunch of cartilage is audible even from my position. He goes down, and she strips his weapon, but fumbles with the safety—not as familiar with firearms as she is with improvised weapons.

One of them is moving behind her while she's focused on the other two. He's got the angle, raising his weapon.

TWO

Sawyer

I DOUBLE-TAP THE MAN WITH A BEAD ON SAVANNAH, HITTING HIS center of mass. The suppressed shots are barely audible over the chaos.

He drops, and suddenly everyone's reacting. One hostile spins toward me, and I put two in his chest, one in his head.

The shots group perfectly—a triangle pattern that drops him instantly. Training takes over, and I'm already shifting aim to the next target, but the third grabs Savannah before I can engage, arm around her throat, using her as a shield.

"Federal agent!" he shouts. "Drop your weapon!"

He's got good positioning—her body blocks most of his center of mass, and he's smart enough to keep his head moving, not giving me a clean headshot. His finger is on the trigger, not in the guard—he's ready to fire.

The laptop taped to her chest makes her torso rigid, harder for her to bend or twist out of his grip.

But I watch her eyes as she processes the situation. No panic, just calculation.

She's testing his stance, the way his weight is distributed. Her hand goes to her ear—casual, like she's in pain. She's thinking, planning, about to do something that's either brilliant or going to get her killed.

Her gaze meets mine across the destroyed apartment. Hazel in the photos, but green in this light, with gold flecks that catch the emergency lighting.

Instead of panic, I see calculation. She goes limp, playing unconscious, while palming something from her ear.

An earring?

The hostile relaxes his grip slightly, thinking she's out.

She drives the earring post into his carotid artery.

The movement is precise—she knows exactly where the artery runs, precisely how much force is needed. The pearl earring disappears into his neck, and for a moment, nothing happens.

Then the blood comes, pulsing with his heartbeat, spraying in arterial spurts that paint the wall behind them. His hands go to his throat, weapon forgotten, and she spins away from him with a dancer's grace.

He's still standing, eyes wide with shock, when I put a round in his head to finish him.

A mercy, really.

Carotid wounds are a bad way to go—conscious for too long, aware you're dying but unable to stop it.

A sudden silence fills the apartment except for our breathing.

Somewhere in the building, a baby is crying. A car alarm goes off outside, probably triggered by the violence. The apartment smells like blood and cordite and the acidic scent of homemade explosives.

One of the attackers is still alive, the one she set on fire, moaning softly from behind the couch. I move over and zip-tie his hands—he'll live, but he's out of the fight.

She stands slowly, the laptop still taped to her body, kitchen knife in one hand, blood running down the other where she gripped the earring too hard. Her chest rises and falls rapidly, but her eyes are steady on mine.

"You're not FBI." Her accent is pure Georgia honey over steel. Not an observation—a statement.

"Guardian HRS. I'm here to get you out." I scan the apartment, checking for additional threats. "Are you injured?"

She looks down at herself, seeming surprised by the blood.

"None of this is mine." Her hand shakes as she sets down the knife, the first sign of reaction. "They killed three agents in the stairwell."

"I saw them." I move closer, noting how she tracks my movement, still ready to fight or run. Smart. "We need to leave. Now. More will be coming."

"I can't—" She gestures to the laptop taped to her body. "This has to stay with me. It's the only proof of what they're planning."

I pull out my knife, and she tenses until she realizes I'm cutting the duct tape, not threatening her. My hands work carefully around the computer, trying not to touch her, but proximity is unavoidable. She smells like fear-sweat and jasmine perfume, an oddly intoxicating combination.

"Ninety-six hours." Her voice is urgent. "They're going to poison the water supply in LA. Tens of thousands will die."

The laptop comes free, and she clutches it against her chest. This close, I can see the exhaustion beneath the adrenaline—dark circles, the hollow of too many missed meals, the particular worn look of someone who's been running on empty.

"Who's 'they'?"

"The Prometheus Network. Domestic terror cell. My partner—" Her voice catches. "My former FBI partner is part of it. He tried to kill me three nights ago."

Sirens wail in the distance, getting closer. I check the window—more black SUVs are arriving.

"We're leaving. Can you run?"

She nods, already moving toward her bedroom. "I need ten seconds."

I follow, watch her grab a messenger bag, and shove the laptop inside, along with a handful of USB drives from a hidden panel behind her dresser. She's planned for this, prepared for running.

"How do we get out?" She slings the bag across her body. "They'll have the stairwells covered."

I move to her bedroom window and check the distance to the adjacent building. "We go out, not down. You afraid of heights?"

Her face pales. "Terrified."

"Then don't look down."

I pull the rappelling gear from my pack and secure the anchor to the reinforced window frame. When I turn back, she's standing there, wide-eyed, breath hitching. The nylon harness dangles from my hands like a promise.

I step in close—closer than I should.

My chest brushes her shoulder as I loop the strap around her waist. She smells like rain-soaked ash and wildflowers crushed under boot soles. My knuckles graze the curve of her hip as I thread the buckle through.

Her breath catches, a sharp sound swallowed by the hum of the storm outside.

"Hold still." My voice comes out lower than I intend. Rough.

Her pulse flutters in her throat as I cinch the strap tight, the movement dragging her hips flush against mine. Heat sparks in the narrow space between us, electric and dangerous.

She looks up, lips parted. Fear and adrenaline blur together in her eyes—and something else, something that burns hotter than the fire waiting beyond the window.

"I can't—" She looks out the window and immediately steps back. "I can't do this."

Footsteps thunder in the hallway. Multiple hostiles, moving fast.

I cup her face in my hands, forcing her to look at me instead of the drop. "Hey. Eyes on me. What's your name?"

"Savi. Everyone calls me Savi."

"Okay, *Savannah*. I'm Sawyer. I'm going to get you out of this, but I need you to trust me for the next thirty seconds. Can you do that?"

She nods, jaw set with determination that probably gets her through most things. Good. She'll need it.

I clip her harness to mine, chest to chest, her arms around my neck. "Close your eyes. Hold on to me. Don't let go."

The door explodes inward. No time for gentle.

I wrap one arm around her waist, grip the rope with my other hand, and step backward out the window.

She doesn't scream, but her arms tighten enough to choke me, her face buried against my throat.

We drop fast, a controlled fall, eight stories in six seconds. Her body pressed against mine, every curve, every tremor, the rabbit-quick beat of her heart against my chest.

We hit the alley hard, and I take the impact on my legs, keeping her upright. "You can open your eyes now."

She pulls back slightly, and we're face to face, inches apart. Her pupils are blown wide, breath coming in pants that ghost across my mouth. Time stops for one impossible second, the world narrowing to green-gold eyes and parted lips.

Gunfire erupts from above, shattering the moment.

I grab her hand, and we run.

A motorcycle catches my eye—a matte-black Triumph parked half in shadow, keys nowhere in sight but tempting as sin.

Agile and quick. Exactly what we need.

I crouch beside it, fingers working quickly and sure beneath the console.

Wires spark, the engine growls to life, low and rough like a warning.

She doesn't ask what I'm doing. Just steps close, eyes steady on mine. When I swing a leg over, she climbs on behind me without a word, her thighs bracketing my hips, palms flattening against my stomach.

The engine vibrates through both of us as I gun the throttle. Her body presses tighter, chest to my back, breath hot against my neck. I don't look back when we tear down the street—because the sound of her heartbeat against my spine tells me she's already all in.

"Hold tight." I kick the engine to life.

"Not letting go," she says against my shoulder blade, and something about the way she says it makes my chest tight.

I weave through late-night traffic. Market Street is empty enough to open up the throttle, the Triumph responding like a living thing. Savannah's weight shifts perfectly with mine as I lean into a turn, her body pressed so tight against mine I can feel her heartbeat through my tactical vest.

The SUVs are back there, headlights in the mirrors, but they're heavy and slow compared to the bike.

I cut through an alley between two restaurants, with trash bins on both sides, leaving barely enough room. Savannah tucks her head against my shoulder, making us smaller. Metal scrapes—my boot catching a bin—but we're through. The lead SUV tries to follow, but crashes as it wedges between the bins.

She's plastered against my back, moving with me through turns, and I'm hyperaware of every point of contact—her thighs pressed to mine, her breasts against my shoulder blades, her hands fisted in my shirt.

Red and blue lights flash ahead—SFPD checkpoint, probably watching for us.

I cut hard right into Chinatown, threading between delivery trucks and late-night vendors.

A night market is still active despite the hour, vendors selling everything from live fish to knock-off electronics.

I weave between the stalls, sending a table of counterfeit purses flying.

The vendor shouts in Cantonese—cursing my entire bloodline, probably. Paper lanterns strung overhead tear as the bike passes underneath, falling like burning snow.

An SUV tries to follow our path but clips a seafood stand. Tanks of live crabs explode across the street, claws clicking on asphalt as they make their escape. The second SUV has to brake hard to avoid the mess, buying us seconds.

Grant Avenue is narrower here, more like an alley than a street. I thread between a delivery truck and a parked car with inches to spare, Savannah's grip tightening as her knee nearly clips the side mirror. She doesn't scream, doesn't distract, just buries her face against my back and trusts me to get us through.

Behind us, engines roar—the SUVs have found us.

"Company," she says in my ear, and I feel her shift to look back. "Three vehicles, gaining."

I accelerate through a narrow alley, sparks flying as the handlebars clip brick walls. We burst out onto Grant Avenue, and I see our problem—another checkpoint ahead, boxing us in.

"Building at two o'clock," she says. "Parking garage, no barrier."

She's right. I aim for the entrance, blow past the ticket booth, tires screaming on polished concrete as we spiral up. The SUVs follow, their bulk slowing them on the tight turns.

Top level—open air, view of the city, and a twelve-foot gap to the next building's garage.

"Oh God." She sees what I'm planning. "No, no, no—"

"Trust me."

I hit the ramp at full throttle. We're airborne, her scream in my ear, the city spread below us like a promise of death if I've miscalculated. The landing rushes up, and we hit hard, back tire skidding, but we're across.

I brake hard, spinning the bike to a stop.

She's shaking against me, but when I look back, she's grinning— wild and fierce and beautiful.

"You're insane," she breathes.

"You're alive," I counter.

She kisses me.

It's sudden, desperate, her hands fisting in my hair as she claims my mouth. She tastes like adrenaline and coffee, and I'm kissing her back before my brain catches up, one hand tangled in her hair, the other pulling her closer.

Heat explodes between us, inappropriate and perfect, and absolutely the wrong time.

"Sorry. I just—adrenaline, and you—" She pulls back, breathing hard.

"Later," I promise, and mean it. Heat coils low in my belly despite everything.

Her lips are swollen from the kiss, and there's a wildness in her eyes that has nothing to do with the jump we just survived. My hand is still tangled in her hair, and I have to force myself to let go. The taste of her lingers—coffee and adrenaline and something sweet underneath, like brown sugar.

"Later." She nods, eyes still on my mouth.

I force myself to focus, checking for pursuit. The SUVs can't make the jump—but they don't need to. Sirens converge on the other building. We have minutes at most.

"Where to?" She settles back against me. The jump, or the kiss, did something to her because she's not shaking anymore.

"Extraction point. Then we figure out how to stop your Prometheus Network."

"Our," she corrects. "Our Prometheus Network. You're in this now."

I start the bike and head for the extraction point. "Yeah, I figured that out when you kissed me."

Her laugh is soft against my shoulder. "That's not why you're in it."

"No?"

"You were in the moment you saw me fighting and decided I was worth saving. Thank you for that."

She's right, but I don't tell her that. Not yet.

The extraction point is a warehouse near the water, but I take the long way, doubling back twice to make sure we've lost pursuit.

Savannah stays pressed against me, and I'm hyperaware of every breath, every shift of her weight.

When I take a hard turn, her arms tighten around my waist, and her lips brush the back of my neck—probably accidental, but it sends electricity down my spine anyway.

Tyler would have liked her.

The thought comes unbidden as we ride through empty streets. He always said I needed someone who could match me, someone who wouldn't be scared off by the life we lead.

"Find a woman who can stab a man and kiss you in the same night," he joked once, drunk after a mission gone sideways. *"That's the one who'll understand you."*

I didn't think women like that existed outside of movies. But here she is, taped laptop and all, having just taken out trained killers with kitchen supplies and grandmother's jewelry.

Tyler, you bastard, you were right about everything.

THREE

Savannah

Seventy-two hours ago, I woke up with Nathan Torres in my bed, his arm heavy across my waist, and thought I knew what my life looked like.

Three years as partners, six months as lovers, and I still got a little thrill watching him sleep. He looked younger like this, without the careful FBI mask he wore during the day. His dark hair was mussed, falling over his forehead in a way that made my fingers itch to brush it back.

"Stop staring," he murmured without opening his eyes, voice rough with sleep.

"Can't help it. You're pretty."

He cracked one eye open, mouth quirking. "Pretty?"

"Beautiful. Devastating. Handsome. Absolutely gorgeous." I traced the scar on his shoulder—a bullet graze from our second year together when a crypto-fraud case went sideways. "How'd I get so lucky?"

He rolled over, pulling me against him, and his kiss tasted like morning and promises. "I'm the lucky one, Savi. Smartest woman in the FBI, and she lets me in her bed."

"Flattery will get you everywhere."

"Good to know." His hand slid down my side, and heat pooled low in my belly. "How much time before work?"

I glanced at the clock. "Forty minutes."

"Plenty of time."

Later, in the shower, Nathan washes my back with the careful attention that made my knees weak.

I thought this might be forever.

We'd talked about it—kids someday, a house outside the city, and normal things that seemed possible despite our abnormal jobs. He'd met my grandmother before she died, charmed her completely. She'd given me her pearl earrings afterward, said, *"That one's a keeper, sugar."*

God, what a fool I was.

Now I'm pressed against a stranger's back on a stolen motorcycle, every nerve ending alive with fear and want, trusting him because the alternative is dying.

The wind cuts cold through my torn blouse as Sawyer navigates San Francisco's maze of streets. I catalog what I know about him: Guardian HRS operator based on the speed with which my desperate call to an old CIA contact for help.

After Nathan destroyed my career, I reached out to my contact. He gave me CJ's name. Said he worked for a group good at extractions.

CJ got Sawyer to me, military trained from the way he moved through my apartment, comfortable with violence in a way that should terrify me, but doesn't.

His body under my hands is solid muscle, coiled power, and he smells like gunpowder and something woody—cedar, maybe pine.

There's a particular way military men hold themselves—spine straight, even when relaxed, awareness of every exit, hands that move with economy. Sawyer has all of that, plus something else—something darker.

The way he killed those men in my apartment was efficient, almost beautiful in its precision. No hesitation, no excess, just the exact amount of violence needed.

It should scare me.

Instead, I feel safer than I have in three days.

His tactical vest has dried blood on it. The thought that he waded through blood to get to me, that he stepped into my war knowing nothing about me except that I needed help, makes my chest tight with something I don't want to examine too closely.

The rappelling rope left his hands raw where he controlled our descent, and I watched him ignore the pain like it didn't exist. There are scars on his forearms—burn scars, old but extensive.

He wears a military challenge coin on a chain around his neck that escaped his shirt during the fighting. Someone else's coin, not his own, which means loss, which means guilt, which means he carries ghosts the way I'm learning to carry betrayal.

"We're clear," he says, voice carrying back to me. "Extraction point's five minutes out."

I should ask where we're going. Should demand credentials, verification, and proof that he is who he says he is. But Guardian HRS is real, and CJ came through.

And more than that, my instincts—the same ones that saved me from Nathan's needle three nights ago—say this man will keep me safe or die trying.

Three nights ago. Thursday. Nathan and I had worked late on the cryptocurrency case, and ordered Thai food to the office like we had a hundred times before.

Nathan was distracted, kept checking his phone, but I figured it was work stress. The Prometheus communications were hidden in the blockchain data we were analyzing, but I didn't know that yet. Wouldn't know until after.

We went back to his place around midnight. Nathan wanted to shower first—said the office air made him feel grimy. I was at my computer, running one more analysis on the blockchain patterns that had been nagging at me all day, when I found it.

Communications hidden in the transaction hashes, using a cipher I recognized because Nathan had shown it to me months ago as a theoretical exercise.

"Hey, babe," I called toward the bathroom, "remember that

cipher you were working on? I think someone's using a variant for—"

The bathroom door opened, and Nathan stood there in just a towel, expression strange. "What did you find?"

"Hidden communications in our crypto case. Look, if you decode the hashes using—" I turned back to the screen, excited by the discovery.

That's when I saw the reflection on my monitor. Nathan behind me, pulling something from his gym bag.

A syringe.

I spun in my chair, already seeing the needle in his hand, the cold calculation in his eyes.

"Nathan?"

"I'm sorry, Savi. You weren't supposed to find that." He moved toward me.

"You're Prometheus." Not a question.

The pieces clicked together—his interest in my decryption work, the way he steered me away from certain blockchain addresses, how he always knew which cases to prioritize.

"It's bigger than you understand. America needs to change, and we're going to change it." He reached for me with the syringe. "This is painless. You'll just go to sleep."

I'd taken Ambien an hour earlier, desperate for sleep after three nights of insomnia over the weird patterns in our case. But it hadn't worked—never does when my mind's racing. So I was foggy but awake, and he thought I was deeper under than I was.

I let my body go limp, eyes fluttering closed. He relaxed slightly, moving closer, and that's when I rolled hard left, off the chair. The needle hit the leather where I'd been sitting.

"Savi!" He grabbed for me, but I was already moving, six years of aikido taking over. I used his momentum against him, a hip throw that sent him into the desk. The lamp shattered, papers flying everywhere.

"Three years," I gasped, scrambling for the door. "Three years of being my partner, six months in my bed, and you were using me the whole time?"

"I love you," he said, getting to his feet, syringe still in hand. "But this is bigger than us. The water supply, the infrastructure collapse, the rebirth—you'd understand if you'd let me explain."

"You're going to kill tens of thousands of people."

"To save millions." He moved to block the door. "The system is broken. We're going to fix it. I wanted you with us, but you're too rigid, too bound by rules."

I grabbed my laptop—instinct more than planning—and my go-bag that I keep by the door. "You don't know me at all."

"I know everything about you. Your coffee order, your favorite movie, how you cry every year on your parents' death anniversary, how you sound when you—"

I threw the coffee mug at his head—my FBI academy mug, ironic—and bolted while he ducked.

Out the door, down the stairs, into the night. Behind me, I heard him calling my name, but it wasn't the loving way he'd said it that morning.

It was cold and professional.

The voice of a stranger I'd been sleeping next to for six months.

The extraction point turns out to be an abandoned warehouse near the water. A helicopter waits, rotors already spinning. The pilot nods at Sawyer, and we lift into the darkness without questions or paperwork. Everything about this screams black ops, off-books, the kind of extraction that doesn't officially happen.

I open my laptop as soon as we're airborne, needing to work, to focus on something besides the heat still coursing through me from that kiss.

Stupid. Reckless.

But when we landed that impossible jump, when death became life in a heartbeat, I needed to feel something besides fear.

"What are you doing?" Sawyer shifts closer to see my screen, and his thigh presses against mine.

"Checking if my distributed backups are intact." My fingers fly across the keyboard, muscle memory taking over.

Seventeen different servers, each containing fragments of the Prometheus data, encrypted with a key derived from my grandmother's birthday, my parents' anniversary, and the GPS coordinates of their crash site—things Nathan knew but would never think to combine.

The encryption is AES-256 wrapped in my own algorithm, something I developed at MIT that never made it into my FBI work because it was too complex for standard implementation.

Server one: intact. Server two: intact. Server three: someone tried to access it six hours ago but failed the authentication. Nathan's digital fingerprints are all over the attempt. He's hunting my backups, but he doesn't know me as well as he thinks.

"I hid pieces of evidence across seventeen different servers, encrypted and fragmented. Even if they find some, they won't get all."

"Smart." Sawyer's approval shouldn't matter, but warmth blooms in my chest anyway. "Tell me about Prometheus."

I pull up the files I've been compiling for three days, ever since I stumbled onto their communications hidden in blockchain transactions I was analyzing for cryptocurrency fraud.

"Attacks on water treatment facilities in Los Angeles. The chemicals they're using will look like standard contamination at first, but it's designed to cause organ failure over time. Thousands dead before anyone realizes it's not accidental."

"You're kidding me."

"I wish I were." I pull up chemical formulas that make my stomach turn. "The genius is in the delayed reaction. Initial symptoms mimic standard waterborne illness—nausea, fever, dehydration. By the time organ failure starts, the victims are scattered across hospitals, with no clear pattern. It'll look like multiple unrelated outbreaks until someone runs toxicology, and by then, the infrastructure panic will have started."

"Economic collapse," Sawyer says, understanding immediately.

"Exactly. Markets crash, supply chains break, government paralysis as agencies blame each other." I show him the Phase Two plans. "That's when Prometheus members, embedded throughout government and law enforcement, step in with 'emergency measures.'

Martial law, suspension of constitutional rights, reshaping America into their vision of what it should be."

"Time frame?"

"Ninety hours from now. Synchronized to hit during shift changes when security is weakest." I show him the decoded messages. "They've been planning this for two years. Nathan—" My voice catches on his name. "He's been feeding them FBI intelligence the entire time."

Sawyer's studying the data, processing fast. "Why water supplies?"

"Maximum fear, minimum trace. It'll look like an infrastructure failure, not terrorism. They want economic collapse, not credit. Let America eat itself alive with blame while they position themselves for what comes after."

"And Nathan Torres tried to kill you when you found out."

It's not a question, but I answer anyway. "I trusted him completely." The words taste bitter. "I went to him when I found the communications. Told him everything. He tried to inject me with something. I'm sure it would have looked like sudden cardiac arrest."

"How did you stop him?"

I remember the moment—the shock of seeing Nathan's face in the darkness, the needle catching the light, the way betrayal felt like ice water in my veins.

"I've been taking aikido since college. Used his momentum against him, threw him, and ran."

"Where have you been for three days?"

"Moving. Different motels, paying cash, staying offline except for essential research." I close the laptop, exhaustion suddenly crushing. "I tried calling FBI headquarters, but they said I was wanted for treason, that I'd stolen classified data. Nathan flipped the narrative. Made me the terrorist."

"But you got word to CIA."

"I have an inside source. He called Guardian HRS for me. Said you could help. I'm glad they called you."

The helicopter banks, heading inland. Sawyer pulls out his

phone and texts someone rapidly. "Safe house might be compromised if they have CIA sources. I'm taking you somewhere else."

"Where?"

"Somewhere they'll never think to look."

I should object, should demand to know where this stranger is taking me. But I'm running on seventy-two hours of broken sleep and constant adrenaline. My body's starting to crash, hands trembling as the fear-chemicals fade. Nathan is hunting me with the full resources of Prometheus and the FBI behind him, and I'm out of options that don't involve trusting someone.

Might as well be the man who jumped out a window to save me.

The helicopter sets down in a clearing near Los Padres National Forest. Sawyer leads me to a hidden vehicle—an old Toyota Land Cruiser that blends in perfectly. "Two hours to the safe house. You should sleep."

"I can't—"

"You're crashing. I can see it. Sleep now while you can. I'll wake you if anything happens."

I want to argue, but my eyes are already closing. The last three days of running catch up all at once, and I barely remember leaning against the window before darkness takes me.

I dream of Nathan. Not the Nathan who tried to kill me, but the one who brought me coffee every morning for three years, who knew I took it with too much sugar and never judged. The Nathan who held me when my grandmother died, who made me laugh at crime scenes, who I thought I'd marry someday.

"No, please—" I must say it aloud because a hand touches my shoulder, gentle but grounding.

"Hey, you're safe. Just a dream." Sawyer's voice pulls me back. "We're almost there."

I open my eyes to find I've shifted in sleep, my head on his shoulder instead of the window. I should move, apologize, but he doesn't seem to mind, and his warmth feels too good to give up yet.

"I was talking in my sleep?"

"You said his name. Nathan." There's something in his tone—

not jealousy exactly, but recognition. "The betrayal hurts worse than the murder attempt."

It's so accurate I flinch. "How do you know?"

"Because you can fight back against someone trying to kill you. Can't fight the memories of when they were someone else."

The challenge coin around his neck catches the dashboard light. "Who did you lose?"

His jaw tightens. "Tyler Brennan. My pararescue buddy. Our helicopter went down in Afghanistan. I got thrown clear, but he was trapped. Fuel tank exploded before I could cut him free." His fingers unconsciously trace the burn scars on his forearm. "Still wear his coin. Reminder that hesitation costs lives."

"Was it your fault?"

"No. RPG hit us; nothing I could have done differently. Doesn't stop me from running the scenarios, looking for the solution that would have saved him." He glances at me. "Nathan choosing betrayal isn't your fault either."

"I should have seen it."

"Based on what? Him being perfect for three years? That's not a failure of observation, Savannah. That's a successful long-term deception operation."

FOUR

Savannah

My full name on Sawyer's lips sends warmth through me. No one calls me Savannah except close friends and family, but it sounds right from him.

"Turn coming up," he says, and I realize I've been staring at his profile in the darkness.

We leave paved roads for dirt roads and climb into the mountains. The trail gets progressively worse until we're crawling over rocks that scrape the undercarriage.

The headlights catch glimpses of a drop-off to our right—hundreds of feet down to tree tops that look like black teeth in the darkness. My hands grip the door handle white-knuckled, and Sawyer notices.

"I won't let us go over," he says quietly.

"How can you be sure?"

"Because you're in the car, and I've decided nothing bad happens to you on my watch."

The certainty in his voice makes something in my chest loosen. This man, who doesn't know me beyond a file and a firefight, has decided I'm worth protecting.

After three days of being hunted by someone who claimed to

love me, Sawyer's straightforward commitment feels like oxygen after drowning.

Finally, he stops at what looks like an impassible cliff face.

"We walk from here."

"How far?" I grab my messenger bag with the laptop, and he pulls a large pack from the back.

"Three miles, mostly vertical." He hands me a headlamp. "There's a fire watch tower that's been abandoned for twenty years. I've been maintaining it as a bolt-hole. No one knows it exists except me."

"Why tell me?"

He looks at me in the darkness, face half-shadowed. "Because you need to know you're safe. And because if something happens to me, you need to be able to get yourself out."

The practicality of it—planning for his potential death—makes my chest tight. "Nothing's going to happen to you."

"Everyone thinks that until it does." He starts up the trail. "Stay close. Some of these drops are fatal if you slip."

The climb is brutal. I'm in good shape from aikido and running, but this is different—scrambling over rocks, pulling yourself up near-vertical sections, every muscle screaming.

The first section is deceptive—a steep trail that seems manageable until you realize it goes on forever, switchbacking up a slope that grows progressively steeper.

My calves burn after ten minutes.

My thighs are screaming after twenty.

Sawyer stays just ahead, occasionally reaching back to help me over obstacles, his hand warm and solid in mine.

"Break," he says at a small ledge, maybe a thousand feet up.

I collapse against a rock, gulping water from the bottle he hands me. Below us, the world falls away into darkness. Above, stars crowd the sky in a way they never do in the city. It's beautiful and terrifying in equal measure.

"You doing okay?" He's not even breathing hard, the bastard.

"Peachy." I wheeze. "Love climbing mountains in the middle of the night while being hunted by terrorists."

"Could be worse."

"How?"

"Could be raining."

I laugh despite everything, and his mouth quirks in what might be a smile.

"Tyler used to say that. Every mission that went sideways, he'd find something that could be worse. *'At least we're not in a swamp.' 'At least no one's shooting rockets at us.' 'At least the food's better than MREs.'*"

"Sounds like a good partner."

"The best." The smile fades. "Until I got him killed."

"You didn't—"

"I hesitated." He cuts me off. "Three seconds of hesitation, trying to find a better angle to cut him free, and the fuel tank blew. Three seconds between him living and dying."

I want to say something comforting, but I understand the weight of those seconds. The moment of Nathan's betrayal, when I froze for just a heartbeat before rolling away from the needle—if I'd hesitated one second longer, I'd be dead.

"Come on," he says, standing. "We're exposed here."

Like before, he climbs just ahead, occasionally reaching back to help me over obstacles, his hand warm and solid in mine.

Then we hit the *actual* climbing section.

"Oh, hell no." I stare at the rock face rising into darkness, the fixed rope line that looks like dental floss against granite. "There has to be another way."

"There isn't." He turns to face me, and in the headlamp's glow, I can see patience in his eyes. "I'll be right behind you. Every step. You won't fall."

"I can't—" My voice cracks. "I'm terrified of heights. Always have been. I can't climb that."

He steps closer, close enough that I can smell the cedar and gunpowder, the clean sweat from our climb. "Look at me, not the cliff."

I focus on his face—the steady gray eyes, the stubble darkening his jaw, the absolute confidence in his expression.

"You fought off trained killers with kitchen knives and chemistry." His voice is low, threaded with quiet awe. "You survived three days on the run with the FBI hunting you. You jumped between buildings on a motorcycle an hour ago. This—" he nods toward the jagged rock face ahead "—this is just granite. One hand, one foot, one move at a time."

"That's different—and technically, you jumped the gap. I just clung on for dear life."

His mouth curves, the memory sparking between us like flint catching flame. "That kiss made it worth it."

Heat crawls up my neck. I try to focus on the cliff instead of the way he looks at me—as if that moment's still playing behind his eyes. The breathless shock of it. The taste of adrenaline and rain and want.

He doesn't tease. Doesn't smirk. Just studies me, thumb brushing over the carabiner in his hand. "I wasn't expecting that," he says quietly.

The confession hangs there, raw and unguarded, heavier than the pack between us. For a heartbeat, neither of us moves. The air smells of stone and storm, thick enough to choke on.

Then he clips the first line into place, voice rougher now.

"Let's get through this climb," he murmurs. "I'm going to attach you to a safety line. Even if you slip, you won't fall far. And I'll be right behind you, close enough to catch you."

My hands shake as he checks the harness around my waist and thighs, professional but careful. This close, I can smell him again— that cedar scent mixed with clean sweat and something uniquely him. Something about his solid presence makes my panic recede slightly.

"Too tight?" He adjusts a strap, fingers brushing my hip.

"No, it's fine." My voice comes out breathy, and not from fear.

He clips me to the safety line, then positions himself behind me. "Climb. I'll guide your feet if you need it."

I reach for the first hold and immediately make the mistake of looking down. The ground drops into a black, endless nothing, and vertigo punches through me. My stomach lurches. My fingers slip. I press myself flat against the rock, breath tearing too fast from my lungs.

"Hey." He's suddenly there, heat and strength at my back, not trapping—shielding. His body brackets mine, his breath brushing my ear, steady and deliberate. "Feel me breathing? Match it. In… out… in… out."

His chest rises against my spine, slow and controlled, each inhale rolling through me like an anchor dropping. I latch onto that rhythm, forcing my lungs to follow. The panic loosens its claws, inch by inch.

But the awareness of him?

That only gets sharper.

His hips press into mine with every breath. His arms cage around me, solid and sure, heat bleeding through my clothes like a wildfire. I can't tell where he ends, and I begin.

"Good girl."

The words hit harder than the vertigo. Low. Rough. A little too intimate. A little too knowing.

Something inside me flips—tight, hot, startling.

Oh.

Oh no.

Oh hell no.

Because the way he says that—like I've already pleased him, like he wants more—does something to me I'm not prepared for. My thighs tighten. My pulse drops straight to my core. And suddenly the climb isn't just about survival.

Suddenly, I want to earn that praise again.

Make him say it.

Hear what other things that voice might do to me when we're not clinging to a cliff.

His hand comes up beside mine, guiding, steady. "Right hand up to that hold at two o'clock."

I reach for it, not because the rock feels safe—but because he does.

Because if I move, if I keep going, if I stay in this moment with him pressed against me, whispering in my ear…

Maybe when we reach wherever the hell we're heading—

He'll tell me I'm a *good girl* again, and I can explore more than that kiss.

Maybe deeper.

Closer.

Hotter.

Maybe I can see what he sounds like when he says *good girl* in a place where he doesn't have to hold anything back.

I move when he tells me to, trusting him to guide my feet when I can't see. His body follows mine up the cliff, never more than inches away. When I fumble for a hold, his hand covers mine, guiding it to the right spot. When my foot slips, his thigh is there, supporting me until I find purchase.

"You're doing good, Savannah. Almost there."

His voice becomes my anchor. The way he says my name—like it belongs in his mouth, like he's tasting it—makes heat curl low in my belly despite the terror.

This is insane.

I'm clinging to a cliff face in the dark, and all I can think about is how his breath feels against my neck, how his body fits against mine like we were designed for this.

"Last push," he murmurs. "Ten more feet."

Those ten feet feel like a hundred. My arms shake with exhaustion, my legs are rubber, but his voice keeps me moving.

"That's it. You're amazing. So strong. Keep going."

When we finally haul ourselves over the last ledge, my knees hit solid ground. I'm shaking—adrenaline, exhaustion, the tail end of fear—but the second my palms meet dirt, relief crashes through me so hard my eyes sting.

"You did it." He drops to a crouch beside me, one big hand rubbing slow circles between my shoulder blades, grounding me. "You climbed that whole thing."

"Only because you were there."

His thumb sweeps once down my spine, deliberate. "No. I just reminded you how strong you are."

I look up at him. Wind-tossed hair. Sweat at his temples. Eyes lit with pride he doesn't bother to hide. A man who's only known me for two hours—but somehow sees straight through the walls I lived behind for three years.

Before my nerves can catch up, I grab a fistful of his shirt and yank him toward me.

The kiss hits like a flare igniting—hotter, deeper, molten.

No hesitation this time.

No shock.

Just want.

Strong enough to steal the breath from both of us.

He growls—low and feral, the kind of sound that vibrates straight through my bones—and then his mouth crashes into mine. Not gentle.

Not careful.

Hungry.

His fingers fist in my hair, tugging just hard enough to rip a breathless gasp from my throat. The other hand clamps at my lower back, dragging me flush against him, holding me in place while he devours me like he's been starving for this from the moment I first touched him.

Heat floods every nerve. I rise into him instinctively, opening for him, chasing every brush of his tongue, every scrape of his teeth.

I'm not shy, not hesitant—I take what I want, take him, because this man pulled me through fire and fear and somehow lit something deeper inside me in the process.

He answers that hunger with more—deeper, harder—his mouth claiming mine like he's mapping me, memorizing me.

His teeth catch my lower lip, a deliberate bite that sends a sharp, hot shock spiraling down my spine. He kisses me like he'd devour the whole moment—devour me—if we weren't on borrowed time.

When we finally tear apart for air, our breaths crash between us —ragged, uneven—like we just hauled ourselves through flames and came out burning.

"We should—" he starts, voice rough enough to scrape.

"Get to the tower," I breathe, lips still brushing his. I let my fingers trail down his chest, a promise more than a touch. "But later…"

The look he gives me says he's already imagining exactly what later means.

"Later," he agrees, and helps me to my feet.

The fire watch tower looms out of the darkness, a wooden structure on stilts that looks like it'll collapse in a strong wind. But when we climb the ladder—me first, him below to catch me if I fall—the inside is clean and well-maintained. Solar battery bank, water filtration system, shelf of MREs, basic medical supplies.

A single sleeping bag, rolled in the corner.

FIVE

Savannah

"Home sweet bolt hole," he says, lighting a camping lantern.

The space is twelve-by-twelve, with windows on all sides, giving a 360-degree view of the mountains. There's a small table, two chairs that have seen better days, a camp stove, and that single sleeping bag that suddenly seems very prominent.

"You can have the sleeping bag," he says, not looking at me. "I'll keep watch."

"You need sleep too."

"I don't sleep much. Occupational hazard." He's already checking window sightlines, cataloging approaches, and shifting into sentry mode.

I set up my laptop on the small table to work and process the Prometheus data while my brain still functions.

Later looms, but for now…I work.

The encryption is layered like an onion, each level requiring different keys. Nathan taught me some of these techniques, not knowing I'd use them against him.

The irony tastes bitter.

Layer three uses a Vigenère cipher variant with a key based on —I stop, staring at the screen.

The key.

It's our anniversary date combined with the coordinates of where we first kissed. Nathan built this encryption using our relationship as the foundation. Either he's more sentimental than I thought, or he's taunting me.

"Bastard," I mutter, typing harder than necessary.

"Problem?" Sawyer glances over from his position by the window.

"The encryption key. It's based on..." I trail off, not wanting to admit how deep the betrayal goes. "Personal information. Nathan's using our relationship as part of the cipher."

His jaw tightens. "He's trying to hurt you even through the code."

"Or he never thought I'd be the one breaking it. Maybe he assumed he'd kill me before I got this far."

Sawyer moves closer, studies the screen over my shoulder. This close, I can feel the heat coming off him, smell that cedar scent mixed with sweat from our climb.

"Can you break it?"

"Already am." My fingers fly over keys, anger making me focused. "He thinks he knows me, but he only knows the version I showed him. The real me is much less nice."

"Good." His hand rests on the back of my chair, not quite touching me but close enough that I feel the almost-contact, like an electric shock. "Nice doesn't survive this kind of betrayal."

Sawyer moves to the window, rifle assembled from his pack, scanning the darkness for threats that followed us.

"How long do we stay here?" I ask, deep into decryption protocols.

"As long as we need to. But..." He turns from the window. "You need to sleep. Real sleep, not catnapping in cars. When's the last time you got more than two hours?"

I try to remember. "Four days ago? Maybe five?"

"That's what I thought." He pulls out the sleeping bag and unrolls it. "Sleep. I'll keep watch."

"You need sleep."

"I'm used to it. Perks of chronic insomnia." He checks his rifle again, movements automatic. "Savannah, let me protect you. Go to sleep."

The words unlock something in my chest. For three days, I've been alone, trusting no one, constantly moving. The idea of sleeping safely while someone else stands guard is almost overwhelming.

I curl up in the sleeping bag, which smells like him—cedar and gunpowder and safety. It's a mummy bag, designed for one person, but surprisingly roomy. Probably because I'm nearly half his size.

The temperature's dropping outside, and even through the down filling, I'm cold.

"You're shivering," Sawyer observes from his position by the window.

"I'm fine."

"No, you're not." He moves from the window, does something to the door—a wedge under it, cans balanced on the handle that will fall if anyone tries to enter.

Early warning system.

"We'll hear anyone coming up the ladder. I can take a break from watch."

He sits next to the sleeping bag, and I shift to make room, but there isn't any. We're pressed together through the down fabric, his body heat seeping through.

"Tell me about Tyler," I say, needing conversation to distract from how aware I am of him.

He's quiet for a moment. "Tyler Brennan. Best PJ I ever worked with. Could find survivors in impossible conditions and had a sixth sense for where people would be. Married his high school sweetheart, had two daughters who look just like him." His voice softens. "He was teaching me to surf. Said I was too rigid, needed to learn to flow with something instead of fighting it."

"Did you? Learn?"

"Never got the chance. Our last mission was supposed to be a routine extraction, a downed pilot in neutral territory. But the intel was wrong. RPG hit us as we were lifting off with the pilot. Tyler was at the door, managing the winch. The explosion threw him back into the cabin, trapping him under equipment that shifted."

I reach out from the sleeping bag, find his hand. He grips it like a lifeline.

"The fuel tank was compromised. I could smell it leaking, and knew we had maybe minutes. The pilots were dead on impact, the rescued pilot was unconscious, and Tyler was screaming. Not from pain—he was telling me to get the pilot out first. That's who he was. Dying, and still trying to save everyone else."

"But you stayed with him."

"I tried to lift the equipment, but it was the gun mount—bolted down, twisted from the impact. I needed tools. Found a pry bar, started working on it, and my hands—" He looks at his scarred fore-arms. "The metal was already hot from the fire starting in the elec-trical systems. Skin just... melted off. But I kept pulling, kept trying."

Tears run down my face, and I don't wipe them away. "How long?"

He leans in, and I meet him halfway—but this kiss isn't like the others.

This one is born from pain and truth and the raw, trembling place he's kept locked for years.

His mouth meets mine softly at first, almost reverent, like he's afraid he might break the moment if he pushes too hard. But then I exhale against his lips, a helpless, aching sound, and something in him snaps loose.

His hand slides from my cheek into my hair, tightening just enough to hold me still as he deepens the kiss, slow but devastating. Not hunger—need. The need to feel something other than guilt. The need to be seen, held, wanted… even in the dark.

"Savannah…" he breathes against my mouth, like my name is the first clean inhale after smoke.

I shift into his lap without thinking, knees bracketing his hips, my hands sliding up his shoulders, over the tense muscles of his neck. The moment I settle against him, I feel it—his body surging up to meet mine in a hard, unmistakable response that steals the air from my lungs.

His breath punches out, sharp and involuntary, as if he hadn't expected the effect I'd have on him—or how fast it would hit. Heat floods through me at the contact, the rigid length of him pressing exactly where I'm already aching. My thighs tighten instinctively, drawing us closer, and his hands clamp around my hips, fingers digging in like he's fighting the urge to pull me tighter still.

The shock in his breath…

The hunger in his body…

It hits me like a spark catching dry tinder—and suddenly staying still feels impossible.

"This okay?" My voice is low, not timid. Offering him control, not distance.

His fingers flex in my hair. "More than okay."

A whisper, rough and honest.

The space between us disappears completely. His lips trail along my jaw, slow at first, then deeper, more urgent. Heat spills through me, pooling low and hard, tightening everything inside me. I tilt my head for him, giving him access, wanting his mouth on my throat, wanting him everywhere.

He kisses down the line of my neck, breath hot against my skin.

"You have no idea what you're doing to me," he murmurs, voice a low scrape that sends a trembling shiver straight down my spine.

I do. God, I do.

Because he's doing the same to me.

My hands slip under his shirt, palms meeting warm, scarred skin. His breath punches out at the contact, and he grips my waist, drawing me closer, holding on like he's afraid I might vanish.

"I shouldn't want this," he mutters against my throat.

"But you do." I press my lips to the corner of his mouth, a slow, deliberate tease. "And so do I."

His forehead rests against mine, breaths mingling, heat wrapping around us in the cramped darkness of the shelter. Something in him softens. Something in me opens—wide, vulnerable, wanting.

He swallows hard. "Savannah… this probably isn't a good idea."

A bitter-sweet truth. His voice is rough with restraint, the kind that costs him something.

"I know," I breathe.

And I do.

I know every reason we should back away, breathe, regroup.

But knowing and wanting are two very different things.

I lean back just enough to put a sliver of space between us—just enough to reach for the hem of my shirt.

His eyes widen, gray gone molten as I peel the fabric upward, over my ribs, over my head, and drop it onto the sleeping bag. The cold brushes my bare skin; his gaze sets it instantly on fire.

His breath catches. "Savannah…"

"I almost died tonight." My voice shakes—but not from fear. From certainty. Want. Need. "Don't deny me this. Not when I'm right here. Not when you're right here."

He stares at me like I'm a cliff he wants to leap from.

Torn.

Hunger battling caution.

Then his resolve cracks.

He lifts a hand, slow as a man touching something sacred, and lets his fingertips trace the curve of my waist. Heat blooms under his touch, a low, spreading ache that pulls a quiet gasp from me. His thumb brushes the underside of my breast, barely there—but I arch into him, inviting more.

"You're sure?" His voice is a rasp.

"Very sure." I grind against him, my knees sinking into the sleeping bag on either side of his hips. The way he inhales—sharp, stunned—sends a thrill through me.

His hands come up, gripping my hips, holding me in place as if he's afraid I'll disappear if he doesn't. The tension in him fractures, the last threads of restraint snapping. He pulls me closer until the heat of him presses exactly where I'm aching for friction.

"Oh God…" he mutters against my collarbone, mouth trailing fire over my skin. "Since you kissed me after that jump, I've been trying not to imagine this."

"Stop trying." I shudder, fingers digging into his shoulders. "Start doing."

SIX

Savannah

His mouth claims mine—slow at first, then deeper, hotter, as if every ounce of fear and grief has melted into want. His hands roam up my back, down my sides, relearning me with every pass of his palms.

My body responds instantly, hips rocking into his, breath catching, pulse pounding hard enough to drown out the storm raging outside.

He teases my lower lip with his teeth, a slow drag that sends a tremor straight down my spine. His voice is wrecked, barely holding on.

"Tell me what you want."

"You." My mouth skims his, breathing the word into him like a vow. "All of you. Tonight."

He exhales hard, forehead dipping to mine, his breath shaking with restraint.

"How do you want me?" His fingers tighten on my hips—testing, hovering on the edge of control. "Hard? Soft? Slow? Tell me."

I lift my hips just enough for him to feel how badly I want this, want him.

"Hard." The word slips out on a shiver. "As hard as you can."

His breath stutters—one heartbeat of disbelief, then hunger surging up to swallow it whole.

"You sure?" His voice drops, darker, rougher. "Because I won't hold back."

"Please don't." I guide his mouth back to mine, my voice threading into his lips. "I want to forget everything except what you're doing to me. Take me there. Take control."

He groans—deep, primal—hands locking around my hips like he finally has permission to do what he's been fighting since the moment we met.

And then he moves—

And I feel the shift in him.

The surrender to the part of himself he's been trying not to unleash.

His chest rises sharply, and he flips us in one smooth motion, laying me back on the sleeping bag, his body covering mine, heat and muscle and restraint stretched thin. His forehead drops to mine, breath trembling.

I pull him down into another kiss—and this time, neither of us holds back.

His hands are everywhere—rough, sure, mapping my skin like territory he's staking a claim on.

Our kiss turns feral, tongues tangling, teeth nipping as I taste the salt of his sweat and the desperation he's been burying for days.

He breaks away just long enough to yank his shirt over his head, the fabric whispering against his skin before it's discarded in the corner of the shelter. Scars crisscross his chest and abdomen, pale lines against tanned muscle, and I trace one with my fingertips, feeling him shudder under my touch.

"Fuck, Savannah," he growls, voice low and gravelly, eyes dark with something primal. "You have no idea what you're unleashing."

"Show me."

His mouth descends again, hot and demanding, trailing down my jaw, my neck, to the swell of my breast. He captures a nipple between his lips, sucking hard enough to make me arch off the sleeping bag with a gasp that borders on a moan. His tongue flicks, teases, then he bites—just a graze of teeth that sends liquid heat pooling between my thighs.

I writhe beneath him, my hands clawing at his back, nails digging in as if to anchor myself to this moment.

But he's not done stripping away the barriers. One hand slides down my side, fingers hooking into the waistband of my pants. He doesn't ask—doesn't need to.

With a swift, possessive tug, he peels them down my legs, taking my underwear with them in one rough motion. The cool air hits my exposed skin, but his gaze devours me, making me feel feverish, wanted, owned. I kick the clothes aside, bared completely now, vulnerable and aching under his weight.

Sawyer pauses, hovering over me, his broad frame caging me in the best way. His eyes rake over my body—slow, deliberate—like he's memorizing every curve, every freckle.

"Look at you," he murmurs, voice thick with hunger. "All mine. Spread those legs for me, baby. Let me see how wet you are for me."

The command in his tone sends a thrill straight to my core. I obey, parting my thighs, and his breath hitches as he takes in the slick evidence of my need. He doesn't waste time—his fingers trace the inside of my thigh, inching higher until he cups me fully, thumb circling my clit with just enough pressure to make stars burst behind my eyelids.

I buck against his hand, a whimper escaping me, but he pins my hip down with his other arm, holding me steady.

"Not yet," he says, his mouth curving into a wicked smile against my skin as he kisses a path down my stomach. "I'm gonna make you beg for it first. Gonna taste every fucking inch of you until you're shaking."

His head dips lower, and then his mouth is on me—hot, insistent, his tongue delving deep and lapping at my folds like a man starved. I cry out, fingers threading into his hair, pulling him closer as he works me over with filthy perfection.

He sucks on my clit, grazes it with his teeth, then thrusts two fingers inside me, curling them just right to hit that spot that makes my vision blur. The shelter fills with the wet sounds of his mouth, my ragged breaths, the storm outside fading to nothing.

"Sawyer—please—" It's half plea, half prayer, my body coiling tighter with every stroke.

He lifts his head just enough to meet my eyes, lips glistening. "Please what? Say it. Tell me you want my cock buried inside you, claiming this pretty little pussy."

The words are crude, filthy, but they ignite something wild in me.

"Yes," I gasp, hips grinding against his hand. "Please fuck me."

That's all he needs.

He rears up, shedding his pants and boxers in a blur of motion, his cock springing free—thick, hard, veins pulsing with the same urgency I feel.

He doesn't tease, doesn't prolong; he positions himself at my entrance, one hand gripping my thigh to hook it over his hip, the other bracing beside my head.

"You're mine," he growls, eyes locking on mine as he thrusts in—deep, unyielding, filling me in one brutal stroke that steals my breath.

I cry out, the stretch burning sweet, and he stills for a heartbeat, letting me adjust, his forehead pressed to mine. But then he moves, pulling back only to slam home again, setting a rhythm that's all power and possession.

His hands grip my hips hard enough to bruise, angling me to take him deeper, harder, each thrust punctuated by the slap of skin on skin.

"That's it," he rasps, voice breaking with the effort of restraint he's no longer bothering with. "Take it. Feel how fucking deep I am. This is what you wanted—me breaking you open."

"Yes!" I meet every thrust, nails raking down his back, lost in the filthy symphony of it—his grunts, my moans, the creak of the sleeping bag beneath us.

He shifts, hooking my other leg over his arm, folding me nearly in half so he can hit even deeper, his thumb finding my clit again to rub in tight circles.

The pressure builds, white-hot and relentless, until I'm teetering on the edge.

"Come for me," he demands, teeth grazing my earlobe, breath hot and ragged. "Milk my cock, Savannah. Show me you're mine."

I shatter—waves of pleasure crashing through me, clenching around him as I scream his name. He follows seconds later, burying himself to the hilt with a guttural groan, spilling hot inside me, his body trembling as he claims me completely.

We collapse together, sweat-slick and spent, his weight a comforting anchor as our breaths slow. He doesn't pull away—instead, he rolls us so I'm draped over his chest, his arms wrapping around me like he'll never let go.

His arms tighten their grip, one hand splaying possessively across my back, the other tangling in my hair as he presses a lingering kiss to my temple. The heat of him seeps into my skin, chasing away the chill of the shelter, and I melt against his chest, listening to the steady thrum of his heartbeat under my ear. It's a rhythm that grounds me, pulling me from the whirlwind of the night into this quiet, intimate space where nothing exists but us.

"You're incredible," he murmurs, voice husky and sated, his fingers tracing lazy circles along my spine.

The touch is gentle now, a stark contrast to the raw hunger from moments ago, and it stirs something deeper in me—a warmth that blooms slow and sweet in my chest.

I tilt my head up, brushing my lips against the stubble on his jaw.

"So are you." My words are soft, but there's a spark in them, an invitation I can't quite suppress.

Even spent, my body hums with awareness of him, of the hard lines of muscle beneath me, the faint scent of sweat and earth clinging to his skin.

His eyes meet mine, that molten gray darkening again as he reads the want lingering in my gaze. A slow smile curves his mouth —predatory, knowing.

"Round two?" he asks, but it's not really a question.

His hand slides down to cup my ass, squeezing firmly, pulling me flush against the growing hardness between us.

I nod, breath catching as I shift my hips, feeling him twitch against me.

This time, it's unhurried, sensual in a way that builds like a gathering storm.

He rolls us again, but gentler, settling between my thighs without the urgency of before. His mouth finds mine in a deep, languid kiss—tongues sliding slowly, exploratory, tasting the remnants of our first frenzy.

I arch into him, hands roaming over the ridges of his scars, memorizing him as thoroughly as he's been memorizing me.

Sawyer breaks the kiss to trail his lips down my neck, nipping softly at my pulse point before moving lower. He lavishes attention on my breasts, sucking and swirling with deliberate patience, drawing out gasps and shivers until I'm writhing beneath him.

"That's it," he whispers against my skin, his voice a low rumble that vibrates through me. "Let me take my time with you."

He eases into me then—slow, inch by inch, filling me with a stretch that's pure, exquisite pleasure.

No slamming thrusts this time; instead, he rocks his hips in a steady, grinding rhythm, each movement deep and controlled, hitting every sensitive spot inside me.

His hands pin mine above my head, lacing our fingers together as he holds my gaze, watching every flicker of ecstasy cross my face.

"Feel that?" he growls softly, his breath mingling with mine. "Every bit of me, made for you. Gonna make you come undone nice and slow."

I do—god, do I.

The build is torturous, delicious, coiling tighter with every measured thrust, every brush of his thumb over my clit. When I shatter, it's with a drawn-out moan, my body clenching around him in waves that pull him over the edge with me.

He buries his face in the crook of my neck, groaning my name like a prayer as he spills inside me again, our bodies locked together in the aftershocks.

We stay tangled like that for what feels like hours, cuddling in the dim light filtering through the shelter's cracks. His arms are a fortress around me, one leg thrown over mine to keep me close, his fingers idly stroking my hair. It's peaceful, intimate—his dominance softened into something protective, tender.

I trace patterns on his chest, content in the silence broken only by our slowing breaths and the distant sound of wind whipping outside.

But eventually, the weight of exhaustion tugs at me. Sawyer senses it, shifting to sit up and gently ease me toward the sleeping bag's edge.

"Bedtime, Savannah," he says, his tone firm, authoritative— alpha through and through. "Get some rest. I'll keep watch."

"Bossy much?" I prop myself on an elbow, eyeing him with a playful challenge despite the drowsiness pulling at my lids.

He smirks, that wicked curve of his lips sending a fresh flutter through my belly. Leaning in close, his voice drops to a gravelly promise.

"Baby, you haven't seen me being bossy yet."

I bite my lower lip, heat sparking in my veins as I give him a look that's all lingering hunger and anticipation—eyes half-lidded, a silent dare that says I'm ready for whatever commanding side he unleashes next.

"Wake me in four hours. You need rest, too."

"I will," he lies, and we both know it.

But I'm already falling, exhaustion pulling me under. The last thing I see is his silhouette against the window, standing watch like he promised, keeping the monsters at bay.

For the first time in days, I don't dream of Nathan. I dream of gray eyes and steady hands, of someone who jumped out a window to save a stranger, of later and all its dangerous promises.

SEVEN

Sawyer

SAVANNAH SLEEPS LIKE SOMEONE WHO'S BEEN RUNNING ON EMPTY FOR too long—deep and still, occasionally making soft sounds that could be distress or just dreams.

I stand watch at the window, rifle ready, but my mind is split between the darkness outside and the woman curled in my sleeping bag.

She's kicked partially out of the sleeping bag in her sleep, one leg exposed, and I force myself to look away from the smooth skin, the curve of her calf.

This is a protection detail. Nothing more. Except it stopped being a protection detail the moment she drove a pearl earring into a man's throat with the same precision I'd use to sight a target.

And the moment I buried myself inside her, broke every goddamn rule in the book—don't fuck the client, don't blur the lines, don't let the mission compromise the man.

But hell, she felt like salvation, and now I'm the one compromised, guarding her with more than just my weapon.

Tyler's voice echoes in my memory: *"You'll know her when you meet her, brother. She'll be the one who makes you want to be better than you are."*

I laughed at him then. Told him that was Hollywood bullshit, that relationships in our line of work were comprised of quick hookups and bitter divorces. He just smiled, that knowing smile that made me want to punch him sometimes.

"Michelle makes me want to come home," he said. "Every mission, every close call, I think about her and the girls, and I fight harder. That's what the right woman does—gives you something worth surviving for."

Looking at Savannah now, hair spread across the pillow I folded from my jacket, I understand what he meant.

For three years, I've been operating on autopilot, taking the highest-risk positions because I had nothing to lose. Now, watching her breathe, I'm already calculating how to keep her alive, how to end this threat, how to give her a life where she doesn't have to look over her shoulder.

Dangerous thinking. Attachment compromises judgment. Caring makes you hesitate. But I'm already compromised, have been since that kiss on the motorcycle that tasted like possibility.

Savannah Cross.

Five hours ago, she was just a name on a mission brief. Now she's imprinted on my senses—the way she felt pressed against me on the motorcycle, how she tasted like coffee and desperation, the fierce intelligence in her eyes as she works through encryption that would stump most experts.

The challenge coin is warm against my chest, Tyler's memory a constant weight.

He'd like her.

Would laugh at how she turned household items into weapons, respect how she fought instead of froze.

He'd understand the sex, too.

I check my phone—encrypted message from CJ. "Safe house compromised. Three-man team hit it twenty minutes after you diverted. Stay dark."

So they have someone inside CIA, or at least inside Guardian HRS's communication chain. Good to know. I delete the message, pull the SIM card, and snap it. From here on out, we're completely alone.

Dawn creeps across the mountains like spilled honey, painting everything gold and shadow. The temperature drops just before sunrise, and Savana shivers in her sleep, curling tighter into the sleeping bag.

I want to go to her, wrap myself around her, share body heat. Instead, I stay at my post, watching the tree line for movement that doesn't belong.

A deer emerges from the forest, then freezes, head up, ears swiveling. Something spooked it. I glass the area with my scope, tracking slowly across the terrain.

There—a glint of metal where there shouldn't be any.

Could be trash. Could be someone's scope catching sunlight.

I watch for ten minutes, patient as stone. The glint doesn't repeat, but the deer doesn't relax either. It bounds away suddenly, white tail flashing.

Savannah shifts in her sleep, the sleeping bag falling away from her shoulders. Her torn blouse reveals the edge of a bruise from where one of the fake FBI grabbed her.

The urge to kill them again, slower this time, surprises me with its intensity.

I've protected dozens of clients over the years—politicians, witnesses, corporate executives. It's always been professional, detached, mission-focused.

This is different.

The moment I saw her fighting in that apartment, something shifted. Maybe it was the intelligence in how she taped the laptop to herself, or the way she didn't hesitate to drive an earring into a man's throat. Maybe it was just recognition—another person who'd been betrayed by someone they trusted, who chose to fight rather than break.

Doesn't matter. What matters is she's under my protection now, and I'll die before I let Prometheus touch her.

She stirs, stretches, and blinks up at me with momentary confusion before memory crashes back.

"You didn't wake me."

"You needed the sleep more than I did."

She sits up, hair messy, the morning light catching the gold flecks in her eyes. "How long was I out?"

"Six hours."

"Sawyer—"

"I've gone longer on less. I'm fine." I turn from the window before the sight of her sleep-warm and soft makes me think things I shouldn't. "Get dressed. MREs in the corner if you're hungry."

She wrinkles her nose but gets up, the sleeping bag wrapped around her shoulders like a cape. The small space means she has to brush past me to get to the food, and the contact is electric.

She smells like sleep and jasmine under the fear-sweat, and I have to focus on the tree line to keep from pulling her against me.

"Beef stew or chicken teriyaki?" she asks, examining the MREs with skepticism.

"Beef stew's from 2019, chicken's from 2020."

"So they're both terrible."

"Pretty much."

She tears open the beef stew with the kind of resignation that comes from having no better options. While it heats, she finger-combs her hair, trying to restore order.

The domestic normality of it—a woman fixing her hair in the morning—clashes with the rifle in my hands and the fact that we're being hunted.

"You're staring," she says without looking at me.

"Scanning for threats."

"Inside the tower?"

"You could be dangerous." My voice is rough as I watch her across the dim shelter, the morning light filtering through the cracks like it's trying to chase away the shadows of last night. "You did stab someone with an earring."

She laughs, and the sound transforms the space from a cold, makeshift hideout to something almost like home—warm, alive, pulling at edges of me I thought were long dulled. It's a bright, unfiltered burst that makes my chest tighten, reminding me why I broke every rule for her.

"Any word from your people?" she asks, still smiling faintly as she stretches, the sleeping bag slipping down to reveal the curve of her shoulder.

"Safe house was hit. We're on our own." The words land heavy, the reality of it settling like lead in my gut. No backup, no extraction —just us against whatever's hunting her. I reach down and grab a harness from my pack, the rough nylon familiar under my fingers. "Here, put this on."

"More climbing?" She eyes the harness with a mix of wariness and that spark of determination I can't help but admire.

"Perhaps." I step into my own harness while she does the same, the straps whispering against her legs as she adjusts them.

I double-check mine first—cinching the buckles tight, testing the fit with a quick tug—professional habit dying hard, even with her. Then I cross to her in two strides, my hands steady as I kneel slightly to inspect hers.

My fingers brush her hips, sliding the straps into place with deliberate care, ensuring they're secure, no give, no risk.

She's close—too close for focus. I stand, and I lean in, unable to resist, my face inches from hers.

Our eyes lock, and I steal a slow, languid kiss, my lips claiming hers with a gentleness that belies the fire still smoldering between us. It's unhurried, my tongue tracing the seam of her mouth until she parts for me, a soft sigh escaping as I deepen it just enough to taste her again—the sweetness from sleep, and that underlying heat that's all her.

My hand lingers on her waist, thumb grazing the exposed skin above her waistband, a promise of more when the time allows.

I pull back reluctantly, the harness now perfectly fitted, and watch as she processes it all—the kiss, the isolation, the weight of what's coming.

"They have someone inside your organization," she says finally, her voice steady but edged with the same realization that's been gnawing at me since the safe house went dark.

"Not Guardian HRS. My bet is on the CIA. Either way, we can't trust anyone except each other."

"Do you trust me?" She asks it casually, but there's weight beneath the words.

I consider lying, keeping it professional. But we're past that. "Yeah. I do."

"Why?"

"Every instinct I have says you're exactly who you appear to be."

"Nathan fooled my instincts for three years."

"Nathan had three years to build a false persona. You've had hours of exhaustion and adrenaline. Hard to maintain a lie under those conditions."

She takes a bite of beef stew that's probably older than she'd like to know. "What about you? How do I know you're trustworthy?"

"You don't." Simple truth. "But I'm the best option you've got."

"That's not very reassuring."

I move closer and crouch in front of where she's sitting. "This morning, watching you sleep, I realized something."

"What?"

"I can't change what happened to Tyler. But I can make sure nothing happens to you. That's not professional, it's personal. You want reassurance? Here it is—I will burn the world down before I let them touch you again."

Her breath catches, eyes searching mine. "That's... intense."

"Too much?"

"No." She sets down the MRE, leans forward until we're inches apart. "It's exactly what I needed to hear."

The air between us charges, and I should move back, maintain distance, keep this professional. Instead, I stay frozen as she reaches out, fingers tracing the burn scars on my forearm.

"Do they hurt?"

"Sometimes. Phantom pain, mostly. The nerve endings remember the fire even though the skin's healed."

She traces higher, pushing up my sleeve to see the full extent. The scars are worst at my wrists and hands, where I gripped super-heated metal trying to free Tyler.

"You held on until you physically couldn't anymore."

"Wasn't enough."

"It was everything." She looks up, and her eyes are bright with unshed tears.

My throat closes. In two years, no one's said that to me. Everyone focuses on the failure, the loss, the what-ifs. She's the first to see the attempt as its own kind of success.

Before I can respond, her laptop chimes. She pulls back, immediately switching to work mode.

"I've broken through another encryption layer." Her fingers fly across keys. "Oh God. Sawyer, look at this."

I move behind her, reading over her shoulder. It's a list of Prometheus Network members—dozens of names across multiple agencies. FBI, ATF, DHS, and even local law enforcement in LA.

"This is bigger than I thought." She scrolls through. "They've been embedding people for years."

"Can you send this to anyone?"

"Not without revealing our location. The moment I connect to any network, they'll trace us." She bites her lip, thinking. "But I might be able to... yes. I can fragment it, hide pieces in multiple locations, set them to auto-release if we don't check in."

"Dead man's switch."

"Exactly. Give me an hour."

She works with absolute focus, tearing into the MRE and methodically portioning out the contents—protein bar first, then the main packet, her movements precise as if she's dissecting a puzzle rather than scarfing down field rations.

I watch her for a moment longer, admiring the way her brow furrows in concentration, strands of hair falling across her face, as if she's oblivious to the world.

I return to watching our perimeter, rifle slung low across my chest, eyes scanning the treeline beyond the shelter's narrow window. The morning is quiet—birds chattering in the canopy, wind rustling the leaves like a soft sigh, nothing human to set my teeth on edge.

No footfalls, no distant engine hum, just the deceptive calm of the wild. But my instincts keep prickling, that low hum in my gut warning me the silence won't hold.

Needing to shake the unease, I move to the edge of the watch tower's platform, the weathered wood creaking under my boots as I lean over the railing. The setup I rigged last year anchors from a reinforced beam here at the top— a thick steel cable stretched taut across the gap to a distant anchor point hidden in the far treeline, the pulley trolley hanging ready, its wheels greased for silent speed.

I test the line, giving it a sharp yank to feel the tension, vibration thrumming steadily up my arms, unyielding but with the perfect flex for a fast drop.

My fingers trace the cable from the beam mount, hunting for frays or slippage in the fittings, then I slide the trolley along a short test span, the faint metallic whisper confirming it's smooth and locked in. Everything holds—secure, a lifeline etched against the sky if we need to vanish into the green below.

Satisfied for now, I unclip and sling the rifle back over my shoulder, scanning the shadows one last time before stepping back inside.

She's still at the computer, but her eyes lift to meet mine, questioning.

We're too exposed here, too stationary. Prometheus has resources and motivation. It's only a matter of time before they find us.

The glint I saw earlier hasn't repeated, but the wildlife patterns are wrong. No birdsong from the west, where there should be morning activity.

The squirrels that were chattering an hour ago have gone silent. Small prey animals know when predators are near.

I count potential approaches—the trail we came up is the obvious one, but there's a ridgeline to the north that a skilled climber could traverse. The eastern face is a sheer drop, but the west has tree cover almost to the tower's base.

If I were assaulting this position, I'd send the main force up the trail as a distraction while a smaller team came from the west.

"There's something else." Her voice pulls me from my threat assessment. "The chemicals they're using—I found the source. They're being supplied by a company called Titan International."

Her voice draws me back inside. "You're sure?"

"Purchase orders, shipping manifests, everything." She looks up at me. "You know them?"

"Yes. If Titan is involved, this isn't just domestic terrorism. There's money behind it, probably foreign."

"We need to stop the chemical shipments."

"We need to stay alive long enough to stop anything." Movement in the tree line catches my eye. "Close the laptop. Grab your bag."

She reacts immediately to my tone, powering down and moving away from the window. She tucks the laptop inside her bag and slings it over her shoulder, while I track the movement—could be deer, but the pattern's wrong.

"What is it?"

"Maybe nothing. Maybe—"

The first bullet punches through the wall two inches from my head.

"Down!" I tackle her, covering her body with mine as more rounds tear through the wooden structure.

EIGHT

Sawyer

THE SHOTS COME FROM MULTIPLE ANGLES—AT LEAST THREE positions, maybe more.

Splinters rain down as bullets perforate the walls. The windows shatter in sequence, glass exploding inward. Savannah is underneath me, her heart racing against my chest, but she's not panicking. Her hands are already reaching for the laptop, making sure it's protected.

"They found us."

"How?"

"Doesn't matter." I pull her toward the trapdoor that leads below. "We're leaving."

More gunfire, from multiple positions. They've surrounded us. I count muzzle flashes—at least eight shooters, probably more. Professional spacing, overlapping fields of fire. These aren't FBI imposters. These are mercenaries.

The first bullet punches through the wall six inches from Savannah's head, showering us with splinters. Then the night explodes.

Automatic weapons fire tears into the tower from multiple positions—muzzle flashes winking like deadly fireflies in the tree line below. Most rounds go wide, distance and elevation working in our favor, but wood shrieks and glass shatters as lucky shots find their mark.

"Move!" I grab her bag with one hand, mine with the other, shoving both into her arms as I push her toward the back door. "Rear deck—now!"

She doesn't hesitate, trusting me even as bullets whine overhead like angry hornets. The tower shudders with each impact, decades-old timber groaning. They're walking their fire up the structure, trying to find our range.

We burst onto the narrow balcony, and Savannah stops so suddenly that I nearly collide with her.

Forty feet below, the forest canopy spreads like a black ocean, treetops swaying in the wind. And stretching from the tower's support beam into that darkness—my emergency egress. A steel cable, finger-thick, angling down into the void, disappearing toward the ridge across the valley.

"That's not—" Her voice cracks. "Sawyer, that's not a rappel line."

"It's a zipline." I'm already pulling the trolley from its hidden mount and checking that the wheels spin freely. "Quarter mile to the landing point."

A burst of gunfire stitches across the railing, sparks flying as bullets strike metal. Savannah drops instinctively, but I keep working —muscle memory from a hundred extractions taking over.

"The angle's wrong for them," I tell her, clipping her harness to the trolley. "They're shooting uphill from eight hundred meters. Half their rounds are hitting trees."

As if to prove my point, bullets crack through the air above us—that distinctive snap of rounds passing close but not close enough. The shooters are good, but physics is on our side.

For now.

"I can't." She's gripping the railing, knuckles white, whole body trembling. Not from the gunfire—from the drop. "It's too high, I can't—"

Another burst rips chunks from the wooden deck. They're

adjusting fire, learning the range. We have thirty seconds before they dial it in.

I step behind her, close enough to feel her racing heartbeat through her back. "You climbed a cliff in pitch darkness," I murmur, securing my harness to hers—tandem configuration, no chance of separation. "You can ride a cable."

"That was different. You were there—"

"I'm here now." I wrap my arms around her from behind, my hands covering hers on the grips. She's shaking so hard I can feel it in my bones. "We go together."

A window explodes somewhere behind us. Glass rains down like deadly snow.

"They're finding the range," I say against her ear, keeping my voice steady even as my mind runs calculations—trajectory, distance, time. "Twenty seconds before they bracket us."

She turns her head slightly, and tears stream down her face. Not from fear of the bullets—from fear of the fall.

"I need you to trust me," I tell her, tightening my arms around her ribs. "One more time."

"I'm scared." Barely a whisper.

"I know. Be scared later. Right now, just hold on."

More impacts—closer now. Wood splinters near her hip. The shooters have found their elevation.

No more time.

I plant my feet, feeling her tense against me. "On three. One—"

Automatic fire rakes the platform.

"Two—"

The railing explodes in a shower of wood and metal.

I don't say three.

I launch us into space.

For a heartbeat, we're suspended—weightless, exposed, perfect targets silhouetted against the stars. Bullets snap through the air around us, one so close I feel its heat kiss my cheek. Savannah's scream tears from her throat, primal and raw.

Then gravity catches us.

The trolley engages with a metallic shriek, and suddenly, we're flying. The cable sings as we accelerate, twenty, thirty, forty miles per hour in seconds. Wind tears at our clothes, our hair. We're skimming through the canopy.

Savannah's hands are locked on the grips, mine covering them, holding her steady as we rocket through the darkness. I can feel her trying not to scream again, her whole body rigid with terror.

"Breathe," I shout over the wind. "I've got you. Just breathe."

We plunge deeper, the cable's angle carrying us down through the forest. Tree trunks flash past in the moonlight—any one of them could be death if we clip it. But I set this line myself, tested it dozens of times. The path is clear.

Behind us, muzzle flashes strobe through the trees—but we're already out of effective range, physics and speed making us impossible targets. The shooting continues, frustrated and futile, as we disappear into the night.

The cable's slow descent carries us over a creek bed, moonlight on water blurring beneath our feet. Savannah makes a sound—half sob, half laugh—as she realizes we're actually going to make it.

"Landing coming up," I tell her, feeling the familiar markers flash past. "When I say, lift your legs."

The terminal tree looms out of the darkness—a massive pine on the opposite ridge, the cable's anchor point fifteen feet up the trunk. The landing platform is narrow, built for one, but I've made it work before.

"Now!"

We lift our legs as the platform rushes up. I absorb the impact through bent knees, using our momentum to swing us around the tree trunk, bleeding off speed. The trolley squeals to a stop against the buffer, and we're suddenly still.

Savannah collapses against me, legs giving out, only my arms keeping her standing. She's gasping, crying, laughing—all at once.

"You're insane," she manages between breaths.

"But alive."

Distant gunfire echoes across the valley—they're shooting at shadows now, or maybe just venting frustration. I unclip us quickly, testing my footing on the narrow platform before helping her down to solid ground.

"Oh God." She drops to her knees in the pine needles, hands pressed to the earth like she's making sure it's real. "Oh God, we just—we flew—"

"Can you run?"

She looks up at me, hair wild, eyes wider. "Better than I can fly."

I almost smile at that. Almost. But then I catch it—the sound of engines starting far below. They're not giving up.

"They'll take the logging road," I calculate quickly. "Try to cut us off at the highway. We go cross-country, stay in the trees."

I pull her to her feet, and she sways slightly before finding her balance. Her hand finds mine, grips tight.

"No more ziplines?"

"Fresh out."

"Thank God."

We plunge into the forest, leaving the cable swaying in the wind behind us. The hunters wanted a kill.

They got a vanishing act instead.

The forest is our advantage. I grew up in mountains like these, learned to track deer with my grandfather before I could properly hold a rifle. But Savannah is a city girl, and she's struggling with the uneven ground.

"This way." I pull her into a drainage ravine, natural cover that breaks the line of sight.

When I rigged the zipline, I needed a fast out and a secure exit. I've mapped this area of the forest and know it well.

Those men will have to trace the zipline to its destination, challenging in the dark, and across two ridges.

But they'll find it eventually. A good tracker will pick up our trail, but I've got that covered, too.

I pull Savannah down a game trail. Her hand finds mine, squeezes. Blood trickles from a cut on her forehead—flying glass or wood, probably.

"You're hurt." I reach for her face, but she catches my wrist.

"Later. We need to move."

She's right, but the blood makes something primitive in me snarl.

They hurt her.

They destroyed my sanctuary and hurt her, and part of me wants to double back, move silently through the trees, and hunt them one by one until the forest runs red.

But keeping her alive matters more than vengeance.

"This way."

I guide her down the slope into a narrow drainage ravine, the walls rising on either side like a natural shield. The moon barely reaches the bottom; shadows swallow us whole.

The ground here is mostly packed dirt and stone—hard, cold, blessedly trackless.

Perfect.

I pull her behind a cluster of granite outcroppings, then crouch, scanning the slope we descended.

"Stay close," I murmur, already moving. "We need to erase everything we can."

I grab a fallen pine bough—long, bristled with needles—and drag it backward over the faint impressions our boots left in the softer soil.

One clean sweep, then another. The tracks blur, vanish, become just another rough scuff in the uneven ground.

I pivot, studying the rock shelf above us. Light-colored chips from our descent catch the faint moonlight. I nudge each one into the ravine with the side of my boot, sending them skittering down the stone chute where thousands of others already lie.

Nothing distinct.

Nothing directional.

Nothing they can follow.

Savannah watches, wide-eyed, chest still heaving from the zipline. "You've done this before," she whispers.

"Too many times." I crouch near her and brush dirt over the last patch of disturbed soil with my gloved hand, flattening it until the surface looks untouched. "Hunters always look for the story the ground tells. So we give it silence."

I step to the ravine's narrow bend, placing my boots directly into the pockets of shadow where the stone is slick and hard—no tread, no trace. "Put your feet where mine go. No edges. No soft spots."

She nods, trembling but steadying, and follows behind me.

I guide Savannah into a deeper cut in the ravine and lower my voice. "We'll hug the stone for the next half mile. No footprints. No scent trail worth a damn. They'll spread out and waste time."

"And us?" she whispers.

I take her hand, guiding it to the cool stone wall. "We disappear."

Then, softer—because she's shaking again and I feel it in the way she presses close:

"They won't find you. Not while I'm breathing."

"There." I spot what I'm looking for—a cave entrance, partially hidden by fallen trees.

"We'll be trapped—"

"Trust me."

We squeeze through the entrance into darkness. I click on my tactical light, revealing a narrow passage that goes deeper into the mountain. I've explored these caves before, mapped them during my bolt-hole preparations. There are three exits, two of which they won't know about.

If they manage to track us to the cave, they'll have an impossible time finding where we exit.

"Stay close." I lead her deeper, the passage narrowing until we're sideways, rock pressing from both sides.

Her breathing is fast, on the edge of panic. "I can't—it's too tight—"

I turn awkwardly and cup her face. "Hey. Look at me. I'm bigger than you, and I fit. You're okay. It opens up just ahead."

She focuses on my eyes, using them as an anchor, the way I taught her on the cliff. We shuffle through, and then the passage opens into a larger chamber. Water drips somewhere in the darkness, an echo telling me the space is significant.

"We can rest here a minute," I tell her, but when I turn, she's right there, closer than expected.

The tactical light throws harsh shadows, making her eyes look darker, the blood on her face stark against pale skin. She's shaking—adrenaline crash, cold, fear, all of it hitting at once.

"You saved my life. Again." Her voice is rough. "That's becoming a pattern."

"It's my job."

"No." She steps closer, and I can feel heat coming off her despite the cave's chill. "Your job was extraction. Everything since has been personal."

She's right.

It's been personal from the moment she kissed me back on that motorcycle. "Savannah—"

I kiss her. Can't not kiss her. She makes a sound that goes straight through me, pressing closer, and I'm lost. My hands tangle in her hair, and hers fist in my shirt, and we're trying to crawl inside each other's skin.

She makes a sound that echoes in the chamber—need and relief and something desperate.

My back hits the cave wall, and she follows, pressed against me from chest to thigh. Heat builds between us, inappropriate and perfect, and absolutely the wrong time. Her leg slides between mine, and I groan into her mouth, control slipping.

"Want you," she breathes against my jaw, and those two words nearly undo me.

"Not here." It takes every ounce of willpower to catch her hands, still them. "Not in a cave while we're being hunted. You deserve better than that."

She makes a frustrated sound that turns into a laugh. "You're too noble for your own good."

"You're too tempting for mine."

I lead her through the cave system, following mental maps laid down years ago. We take passages no one would think are passable, moving steadily toward the exit that opens a mile from where we entered.

"How did they find us?" She asks as we navigate a particularly narrow section.

"Satellite surveillance, maybe. Or they've been checking all the abandoned structures in the area." I pause at a junction, choosing the left passage. "Doesn't matter now. What matters is they showed their hand—they want you dead, not captured."

"Because I have the evidence."

"Because you're the only one who can decode it fully." I help her over a rock formation. "Kill you, destroy the laptop, and Prometheus continues as planned."

Light ahead—natural, not artificial. The exit. I motion for silence, move forward to scout.

The opening is clear—no movement—but that means nothing.

"Stay here," I tell her. "I'm going to check—"

"No." She grabs my arm. "We stay together. You promised."

I want to argue, but she's right. I did promise. "Together then. But you stay behind me."

We exit the cave carefully, and I scan for threats. Nothing immediate, but the forest is too quiet. Birds should be singing. Their silence means predators.

"We need to get to a vehicle," I tell her. "There's a ranger station four miles northeast. They'll have trucks."

"Can we make four miles?"

"We have to."

We move through the forest, using game trails and natural cover. She's naturally learning by watching me, moving quietly, and placing her feet where I place mine.

Every hundred yards, I stop to listen, check our six, and make sure we're not walking into an ambush.

Two miles in, she's flagging. Adrenaline crash, exhaustion, the accumulated stress of four days running. She stumbles, and I catch her.

"I'm fine," she lies.

"You're not." I scan our surroundings, spot what I need. "That deadfall. We'll rest for ten minutes."

"We don't have time—"

"Ten minutes won't matter if you collapse." I guide her to the fallen tree and make her sit. "Drink." I hand her my water bottle.

She drinks, hands shaking slightly. "I'm not usually this weak."

"You're not weak. You're human. There's a difference." I check her for injuries I might have missed, and find bruises blooming on her ribs from our hard landing. "Anything broken?"

"No. Just sore." She looks up at me, and there's something vulnerable in her expression.

A branch snaps fifty yards away.

I pull her down behind the deadfall, hand going to my weapon. Through the gaps in the wood, I see them—two men in tactical gear, weapons ready, sweeping our trail.

They're going to find us. The cover's not good enough, and we can't run without being seen.

"Stay down. No matter what happens, stay down."

"Sawyer—"

I'm already moving, rolling out from cover, and engaging. My first shots take the nearest shooter center mass, spinning him down. The second dives for cover, returning fire that chews bark from trees inches from my position.

I flank left, forcing him to track me, drawing his attention from where Savannah hides. He's good, professional, but I'm motivated.

He's hunting for money.

I'm protecting someone who matters.

The dance is familiar—move, shoot, cover, repeat. I take a graze across my ribs that burns like fire, but it gives me the angle I need. Three rounds, tight grouping, and he's down.

"Clear," I call, and Savannah emerges from behind the deadfall.

She sees the blood immediately. "You're hit."

"Graze. I'm fine."

"You're not fine, you're bleeding." She's at my side, pulling up my shirt to examine the wound. "This needs treatment."

"Later."

"No, now." She tears strips from her already-ruined blouse. "Sit still."

"Where did you learn field medicine?"

"Red Cross volunteer in college. Seemed like a useful skill." She ties off the bandage, gentle but efficient. "This'll hold until we can do better."

"We need to move. Those shots will bring more." More concerning is how they found us so quickly.

She helps me up, and I notice she's taken one of the dead mercenaries' weapons—a compact HK416.

"You know how to use that?"

"Point and squeeze, right?" At my look, she smiles grimly. "Daddy was a Marine. I've been shooting since I was a kid. Just never shot at people before today."

We move faster now, urgency overriding exhaustion. The ranger station appears through the trees, and miracle of miracles, there's a truck parked outside.

"Wait." I hold her back, studying the scene. "Too easy."

But scans reveal nothing, and we're out of time. More voices behind us, closing fast.

"We go fast," I tell her. "I'll cover, you get the truck started."

She nods, and we break from cover together. No shots, no ambush. Maybe luck's finally on our side.

The truck's unlocked—rangers up here don't expect theft. Savannah finds the keys, and the engine roars to life.

"Go, go, go!"

I dive in as she accelerates, tires spinning on gravel. In the mirrors, figures emerge from the forest, muzzle flashes, but we're already around the bend, gaining speed.

"Where to?" she asks, hands steady on the wheel despite everything.

"South. Los Angeles." I pull out her laptop, praying it survived the chaos. It powers on, and relief floods through me. "We've got thirty-six hours to stop Prometheus. Time to go on offense."

"How?"

"You've got their membership list. We're going to start dismantling their network, one member at a time."

She glances at me, something fierce in her expression. "Together?"

"Wouldn't have it any other way."

NINE

Savannah

THE TRUCK SMELLS LIKE PINE AIR FRESHENER AND OLD COFFEE, rattling with every pothole as I push it faster than it wants to go down the mountain road. Sawyer works on my laptop in the passenger seat, his blood seeping through the makeshift bandage I applied, and I'm trying not to think about how close those bullets came to taking him from me.

Which is insane. I shouldn't feel like losing him would break something fundamental in me.

But here's the thing about trauma—it strips away all the careful constructions we build around ourselves. The polite distances, the professional boundaries, the measured responses.

When someone saves your life, when you trust them with your survival, when they bleed for you, the typical timeline for emotional connection gets thrown out the window.

I've known Sawyer for maybe a day, but I've seen him kill for me, take bullets for me, jump from a tower with me in his arms. That's more truth than three years with Nathan ever revealed. Nathan showed me what he wanted me to see. Sawyer has shown me who he is when everything is on the line.

And God help me, I want him with an intensity that scares me.

"Take the next left," he says, not looking up from the screen. "Service road, stays off main highways."

I make the turn, tires skidding on loose gravel. In the mirrors, no pursuit yet, but they'll be coming.

"Do you have any backups?"

"Yes. I uploaded a dead man's switch. The evidence is distributed across seventeen servers, all set to release in"—I check my watch—"thirty-four hours if I don't input the stop code."

He goes quiet. Too quiet.

He reaches back for my messenger bag. "Anything on this you can't afford to lose?"

My brain stutters. Years of research. Case files. "The evidence—"

"You said you distributed it across seventeen servers."

"Right. I can patch it back together from anywhere."

Before I can process why he's asking, my phone sails into the darkness.

"Sawyer!"

The laptop follows, disappearing into the brush.

"What the hell are you doing?" I'm half-shouting, watching years of my life vanish.

The messenger bag goes last—he checks it once more, dumps a charging cable and notepad, then sends it flying. Window up. Done. Maybe ten seconds total.

"Making sure they can't follow us." He settles back like he didn't just erase my entire digital footprint. "We'll get you a clean device when we're clear."

My hands shake on the wheel. He's right—I know he's right—but the absolute certainty, the zero hesitation...

And God help me, that makes him even sexier.

"Eyes on the road," he says quietly. There's something in his voice that says he knows exactly what I'm thinking.

"That's assuming we're not dead in thirty-four hours."

"We won't be." The certainty in his voice makes me believe him. He winces as we hit a pothole, hand going to his ribs.

"You need a hospital."

"I need to keep you alive."

"Those aren't mutually exclusive."

We drive for a while longer, but eventually the forest road dumps out onto a highway. At the first town, I spot a pharmacy.

"We're stopping."

"Savannah—"

"Non-negotiable." I pull in and park behind the building where we're not visible from the road. "Five minutes. We need medical supplies."

The normalcy of the pharmacy—fluorescent lights, muzak playing "Girl from Ipanema," a bored teenager at the register—feels surreal.

I grab a basket and move fast through the aisles: antibiotic ointment, bandages, surgical tape, and pain meds. My fingers shake as I reach for hydrogen peroxide, remembering the blood flowing from Sawyer's wounds.

The hair dye display catches my eye. If they're tracking us through cameras, we need to change our appearance. I grab black for him, auburn for me, and a pair of scissors. The teenager doesn't even look up from his phone as I pay cash.

Back at the truck, Sawyer climbs into the driver's seat.

I don't argue, sliding into the passenger side.

We're back on the road until Sawyer pulls into a rest stop. "I need to treat this." He points to his side where fresh blood seeps through his shirt.

The bathroom is grimy, fluorescent light flickering, and smells like industrial cleaner and desperation. But it has running water and a lockable door. Sawyer peels off his shirt, and I forget to breathe for a second.

His torso is a map of violence—old scars layered under fresh bruises, the new graze angry and red against tan skin. But it's the body underneath that makes heat pool in my belly.

Functional muscle, not gym-pretty but earned through use. A dusting of dark hair across his chest. Hip bones that cut sharply above his tactical pants.

"You're staring," he says, mouth quirking.

"You're hurt." I force myself to focus on medical, not the way I want to trace every scar with my tongue.

The graze is deeper than I thought, still seeping blood, and his entire right side is purple-black with bruising. "This is going to hurt," I warn, cleaning the wound with antiseptic.

"I've had worse." But his jaw clenches, muscles tensing under my hands.

I work as gently as I can, hyperaware of his skin under my palms, the way his breathing changes when I hit a particularly tender spot. This close, I can smell him—gunpowder and sweat and that cedar scent that's becoming familiar.

"Some of these scars are recent."

"Occupational hazards. Guardian HRS doesn't exactly handle easy cases."

"And the burn scars?" I trace one that wraps around his ribs, feeling him shiver under the touch. "All from the crash? Did anyone else…" I can't finish the question, and realize I probably shouldn't have asked.

"I was the only survivor."

"Survivor's guilt is a hell of a thing."

"Speaking from experience?"

"My parents died in a car accident when I was seven. I was in the back seat, and walked away without a scratch." I tape down the fresh bandage, letting my hands linger perhaps longer than necessary. "Spent years wondering why I lived when they didn't."

"Find an answer?"

"No. But I found a purpose. That's almost as good." I help him back into his shirt. "Your turn. Why did Tyler's death hit you so hard? You said it wasn't your fault."

He's quiet for a moment, and I think he won't answer. Then: "Because he had kids. Two little girls who'll grow up without their father because I couldn't get him out. Every month I send money to his widow, and every month she thanks me, not knowing I'm the reason she's alone."

"You're not—"

"I know. Logically, I know. But logic doesn't stop the dreams where I save him. Where I'm faster or stronger or just... enough."

I cup his face, force him to look at me. "You are enough. You've saved me three times and counting. You're enough."

Something shifts in his eyes, and then he's kissing me, desperate and deep. When we break apart, we're both shaking.

"We should go," he says roughly. "They'll track the truck soon."

He pulls me close, and I realize it's not about desire—he's checking the parking lot over my shoulder. "Two vehicles just pulled in. Could be nothing."

"What do we do?" Fear knots my stomache, gripping hard.

"We walk out casually. Couple on a road trip." He takes my hand, interlacing our fingers. "If they move on us, you run for the truck. Don't look back."

"We've discussed this. I don't leave you behind."

"And I don't let you die for me."

The two vehicles—black SUVs with tinted windows—are parked strategically to block exit routes. Definitely not a coincidence.

"Keep walking," Sawyer murmurs, thumb stroking my hand.

Four men exit the SUVs, trying to look casual, but their tactical boots and concealed weapons give them away. They're moving to surround us.

"When I say run—"

I don't let him finish. Instead, I stop abruptly, pull him down for a loud, public kiss, and use the movement to slip the compact pistol from his waistband. When I break the kiss, I whisper against his mouth, "Trust me."

Then I'm moving, not away but toward the nearest hostile, stumbling like a drunk girl. "Oh my God, is that a real Rolex? My daddy collects watches—"

I'm inside his guard before he processes the threat. The pistol presses against his kidney as I use his body to shield mine. "Nobody moves, or your friend discovers what his spine looks like."

The tactical advantage shifts in seconds. Sawyer's already moving, flanking the others while they're focused on me. God, we work well together—no communication needed, just instinct and trust.

The other three freeze, hands hovering near weapons.

"Smart girl," my hostage says. "But you're outnumbered."

"I'm also desperate, which makes me dangerous." I press harder, making him grunt. "Here's what's happening. You're going to tell your friends to back off. We're taking your vehicle. Anyone who follows, I shoot."

"You won't get far—"

Sawyer's moved while I held their attention, and now has his weapon trained on the others. "She's not bluffing. I've watched her kill three men today. She's getting creative."

I push my hostage forward, keeping the gun on him. "Keys."

He tosses them to Sawyer, who's already moving to the nearest SUV. I back toward it, maintaining aim.

"This isn't over," one of them calls.

"No," I agree, sliding into the passenger seat as Sawyer starts the engine. "But you just lost this round."

We peel out, and I expect gunfire, but none comes. They want us alive now, probably to find out what we know.

"That was risky," Sawyer says once we're on the highway.

"It worked."

"You could have been killed."

"So could you. That's why we're a good team."

I need to focus on something besides the adrenaline making my hands shake.

"I know what we need to do."

"What?"

"Break into Titan's logistics hub and destroy their chemical supply."

He glances at me. "That's insane."

"You said it yourself—offense is the best defense. Besides, who would be crazy enough to attack Titan on their home turf?"

"You, apparently."

"What else are we going to do. If we do nothing, people die."

"*We* aren't doing this."

"I'm done running. It's time to hit back."

"Savannah…"

"You said you'd burn the world down to protect me. Let me burn their world down to protect everyone else."

He laughs, dark and appreciative. "You're different than your file suggested."

"What's that?"

"Spunky. Fearless. Ferocious."

"Well, I'm alive, and very pissed off."

Sawyer studies me for a long moment, something shifting in his expression. "You're serious about hitting Titan."

"Dead serious." I meet his gaze. "They're supplying chemicals to poison water supplies. We have their location, their security layouts. We can stop this."

He pulls out his encrypted phone, decision made. "You're right about going on the offense. We're just not doing it alone."

"What does that mean?"

"I'm getting us an army." He hits a speed dial. "You want to burn their world down? Let me introduce you to the people who do that for a living."

TEN

Savannah

─────────

SAWYER MAKES A CALL, HIS VOICE SHIFTING TO MILITARY EFFICIENCY. Not one word wasted.

"CJ, I've got Savannah Cross, but we have a situation." He pauses, listening. "Domestic terror attack…Prometheus is planning to poison LA's water supply…Affirmative…day after tomorrow."

Another pause. His jaw tightens.

"Titan International. LA facility. Cross has the whole thing decoded—chemical compositions, everything." He glances at me. "She wants to hit Titan, and honestly? She's not wrong."

He listens, then actually smiles slightly.

"Yeah, she's different. Took out four hostiles with kitchen knives and an earring... I'll explain later." Another pause. His expression darkens at whatever CJ says next. "They've got teams hunting us. Already had three engagements." He looks at the bruising on my arms. "We're both functional, but we could use some downtime… Copy that." He ends the call and looks at me.

"You called in backup?"

"I called in the cavalry." His hand finds mine on the gear shift. "You're not wrong about hitting Titan, but we're not doing it alone. My teammates will meet us tomorrow."

"Tomorrow?"

"They need time to prep, and we need downtime."

"Downtime? We don't have any time to waste."

"Savannah... These people are the best of the best. If you want this done and done right, let them do what they do best. Right now, our orders are to rest and recover while they build out a mission. I trust them with my life."

"So what's the plan?"

"CJ is activating the troops. They need a day to organize. We'll meet up with them in the morning."

"What do we do until then?"

"Our orders are to rest and recuperate."

"Rest and recuperate?"

"Yeah." He reaches over and squeezes my thigh. "First, we'll replace your laptop, then we'll find a motel close to LA, clean up, eat something, and rest."

After a quick stop to pick up a new computer, grab a change of clothes, and other things, Sawyer finds a motel an hour north of LA. The kind of place that takes cash and doesn't ask questions. Two stories of peeling paint and broken dreams, but it's off-grid and has multiple exits. Sawyer secured us a room while I waited in the SUV, baseball cap pulled low.

"Teams arrive tomorrow," he says, closing the door behind us. "That gives us a few hours."

The room is small—one bed, an ancient TV, and a water stain on the ceiling that looks like a map of somewhere unpleasant. But it's safe, and after what feels like days of running, safe feels like luxury.

I set my new laptop on my lap, needing to keep working, but Sawyer takes it from my hands.

"You need rest."

"I need to finish decrypting—"

"You need to stop for five minutes." His hands cup my face, thumbs brushing my cheekbones. "You're running on adrenaline. You'll be useless you rest."

"I don't know how to stop." The admission comes out broken. "If I stop moving, stop working, I have to think about—"

"Nathan."

The name hangs between us like a blade.

"Four nights ago, I was in his bed. I thought I knew him. Thought I loved him." Tears burn my eyes. "How did I miss it? How did I share my body with someone capable of mass murder?"

Sawyer pulls me against his chest, and I break. Three days of fear and betrayal pour out in ugly sobs that shake my whole body. He holds me through it, solid and steady, one hand in my hair, the other rubbing circles on my back.

"It's not your fault," he murmurs against my temple. "He was trained to deceive. Three years of deep cover—that's professional-level manipulation."

"But I should have—"

"No." He pulls back, forces me to meet his eyes. "You trusted someone you had every reason to trust. That's not weakness, that's human."

"I'll never trust anyone again."

"You trust me."

It's not a question, but I answer anyway. "You're different."

"Why?"

"Because you bled for me before you knew my name. Because you saved me. Because you've had a dozen chances to betray me and haven't."

"Or maybe," his voice drops, rough and warm, "because sometimes you know. Sometimes you meet someone and every instinct says 'this one, this is real.'"

The air between us charges. We're so close I can see the gold flecks in his gray eyes, feel his breath on my lips.

"Sawyer..."

"I know." His forehead rests against mine. "Wrong time, wrong place, wrong everything."

"But right person?"

"Yeah." The word is barely a breath. "Right person."

I should pull back. Should be professional. Should remember that trauma isn't the best way to begin a relationship.

Instead, I kiss him.

It's different from the desperate kisses before—slower, deeper, exploratory. His hands tangle in my hair while mine find the hem of his shirt. When I trace the bandage I applied earlier, he groans into my mouth.

"We should stop and sleep," he says against my lips.

"We should," I agree, pulling his shirt over his head.

The scars are silver in the dim light, a map of survival I want to memorize with my fingers. When I trace the burn on his ribs, he shudders.

"Savannah..."

"I need this," I whisper against his throat. "I need something real, something that's just ours, something Nathan never touched."

He pulls back to study my face, searching for doubt. Whatever he sees makes him nod slowly.

"Okay. But we do this right." He frames my face with his hands. "This isn't adrenaline or trauma. This is me wanting you. Has been since you took down that merc with an earring."

"That's what does it for you? Violence?"

"Competence." He kisses me again, slow and thorough. "Strength. The way you refuse to break."

His hands are gentle as they undress me, reverent in a way Nathan's never were. Every scar gets kissed, every bruise acknowledged. When he finds the mark Nathan left on my hip—fingerprints from when he grabbed me—something dark flashes in his eyes.

"I'll kill him for this."

"Later." I pull him down for another kiss. "Now, make me forget him."

And he does.

His mouth claims mine, hot and demanding, and he traces a path down my throat, each kiss a promise, each touch erasing the memory of hands that lied.

Where Nathan took, Sawyer gives. Where Nathan rushed, Sawyer savors.

"Look at me," he murmurs against my collarbone. "I need to see you."

I open my eyes and meet his gaze. The intensity there steals my breath—desire mixed with something deeper, something that makes my chest ache.

"There you are," he whispers, cupping my face. "Stay with me. This is us. No one else exists right now."

He kisses me again, and I arch into him, needing to be closer. My hands map the terrain of scars across his back, each one a story of survival, of the man who jumped buildings to save me.

When his palm skims over my breast, I arch into his touch, desperate for more. He takes his time, thumb circling until I'm writhing beneath him, small sounds escaping that I've never made before.

"So responsive," he murmurs against my throat, teeth grazing the sensitive spot where neck meets shoulder. "Want to find every place that makes you shake."

His mouth follows his hands lower, tongue tracing my collarbone, the valley between my breasts, the sensitive underside that makes me gasp. He lavishes attention on each nipple until they're peaked and aching, until I'm pulling his hair, unsure if I'm pushing him away or begging for more.

"Sawyer, please—"

His tongue swirls around my navel.

"Oh God—"

"Savannah." My name is a prayer on his lips as he moves lower, tongue tracing patterns that make me gasp. "Beautiful. So damn beautiful."

He takes his time, mouth and hands worshipping every inch of skin until I'm trembling, fingers twisted in his hair. Nathan was always perfunctory, goal-oriented. Sawyer seems determined to memorize my body's every response.

"Please—" The word breaks from me when he finds that spot behind my knee I didn't even know was sensitive.

"Not yet." His voice is rough with control. "I want to know everything. Every sound you make, every way you move."

His mouth travels higher, and when he reaches the apex of my thighs, I cry out, back arching off the bed. He holds my hips steady, relentless in his attention.

He proves he's a man of action, not just words. His mouth finds me already wet and wanting, and the first stroke of his tongue makes me cry out. Nathan never—God, Nathan never did this, said it was unnecessary. But Sawyer acts like he's been starving for it, for me.

His hands grip my thighs, holding me open as he devours me with single-minded intensity. When he slides two fingers inside, curling them just right while his mouth continues its assault, I shatter embarrassingly fast, my whole body convulsing.

"Beautiful," he breathes against my inner thigh, pressing kisses to oversensitized skin. "Again."

"I can't—"

But he proves me wrong, fingers and tongue working together until I'm climbing again, higher this time. He adds a third finger, the stretch perfect, and when he crooks them while sucking hard.

I scream. Actually scream, back bowing off the bed, fingers twisted in his hair as waves of pleasure crash over me.

He doesn't stop, doesn't slow, just gentles his touch as he works me through it, drawing out every aftershock until I'm boneless and gasping.

When he finally kisses his way back up my body, I can taste myself on his lips—earthy and intimate—intimate in a way that makes me blush.

"The way you come apart," he breathes against my mouth. "I want to see it again. And again."

"Sawyer, I need—" My hands fumble with his belt, desperate to touch him. "Now. Please."

He helps me, shedding the last of his clothes, and when I wrap my hand around him, his control finally cracks. The sound he makes—half growl, half prayer—sends heat spiraling through me.

This is Sawyer, only Sawyer.

I stroke him base to tip, learning what makes his breath catch, what makes his hips jerk. When I twist my wrist on the upstroke, his control snaps.

"Savannah—" He catches my wrist. "If you keep that up, this'll be over before it starts." He catches my wrists and pins them above my head with one hand. "Enough. My turn. Eyes on me," he commands, and I force them open. "Want to watch you take me."

He pushes in slowly, so slowly, and the stretch is intense, almost too much. I'm still swollen and sensitive from two orgasms, and every inch feels like fire and perfection.

"So tight," he grits out, jaw clenched with control. "So perfect. Made for me."

He watches my face, and the stretch, the fullness, the rightness of it makes us both gasp. For a moment, neither of us moves, overwhelmed by the connection.

When he's finally, fully inside, we both need a moment. I've never felt so full, so complete. He releases my wrists to frame my face with both hands, and the tenderness in the gesture contrasts beautifully with the raw possession of him inside me.

"Perfect," he breathes. "You're perfect."

"Please move."

He does, pulling out almost completely before sliding back in, setting a rhythm that builds slowly. Each thrust goes deeper, hits differently, and when he shifts my hips, angling up—

"There! Oh God, right there!"

He grins, fierce and male. "Found it."

He hits that spot with devastating accuracy, over and over, until I'm climbing again, impossible as it seems. His thumb finds my clit, circling in time with his thrusts, and the dual sensation is overwhelming.

I wrap my legs around his waist to pull him closer. One hand threads through mine against the pillow while the other grips my hip, angling me until—

"Oh God, right there—"

"I've got you." His rhythm never falters, building me back up with devastating precision. "Let me see you fall apart again."

His words are my undoing. I clench around him, my third

orgasm rolling through me in waves that seem endless. He curses, thrusts going erratic, and then he's following me over, my name a broken prayer on his lips.

But he's not done.

The angle, the friction, his thumb finding exactly the right spot—it's too much and not enough. I'm climbing higher, faster, and when he shifts slightly, hitting deeper, I break.

He stays hard inside me—how is that even possible?—and rolls us so I'm on top, straddling him. From this angle, he's even deeper, and I gasp at the sensation.

"Want to watch you ride me," he says, hands gripping my hips.

I've never been on top—Nathan always insisted on control—but Sawyer's eyes are hot with encouragement, with need, with something deeper than lust.

I start tentatively, rolling my hips experimentally, but when his head drops back, and he groans, I grow bolder. I find a rhythm, rising and falling, taking him deep. His hands cup my breasts, thumbs circling my nipples, and the combination of sensations has me climbing yet again.

"That's it," he encourages, one hand sliding down to where we're joined. "Take what you need."

When his thumb presses firmly on my clit while I grind down, taking him to the hilt,

"Come for me," he demands, voice rough. "Let me feel you."

I come apart completely. This orgasm is different—deeper, more intense, pulling from my core. He wraps his arms around me as I shake apart, and then he's coming too, face buried in my neck, my name reverent on his lips.

My name is rough and reverent on his lips as he buries his face in my neck. We cling to each other, trembling through the aftershocks, neither willing to let go.

When he tries to move, I hold him tighter. "Not yet. Please."

He stays, taking his weight on his elbows but remaining close, still inside me. His forehead rests against mine, and we breathe the same air, hearts gradually slowing to match.

"That was..." I can't find words.

"Yeah." He kisses me softly. "It was."

We lie tangled in damp sheets, my head on his chest, listening to his heartbeat. His fingers trace lazy patterns on my spine while mine map the scars on his ribs. I'm deliciously sore in all the right places, my body still humming from his attention.

I'm completely wrecked—muscles like jelly, body still pulsing with aftershocks. I've never come four times in my life, let alone in one session.

"Nathan never—" I start, then stop. "Sorry. I shouldn't compare."

"Say it." His voice rumbles under my ear. "Whatever you need to say."

"Is it... is it always like that? Nathan treated sex like a transaction. Efficient. Goal-oriented. He never..." I trace the burn scar that wraps around his ribs. "He never made me feel wanted. Just convenient."

"Never?"

"Never."

"His loss." Sawyer tilts my chin up. "You're not convenient, Savannah. You're essential."

The weight of that admission hangs between us. This thing between us—it's not just adrenaline or proximity. It's something rare, something worth fighting for.

The word hits me in the chest, and I kiss him to avoid the emotions threatening to spill over.

Hours later, we're tangled in sheets that smell like hotel detergent and us. Sawyer traces lazy patterns on my shoulder blade while I scroll through delivery options on my new phone.

"Thai or pizza?" I ask.

"You pick."

"That's a cop-out answer."

"I'm not picky." His hand slides down my spine. "But I am hungry."

I order Thai because the pizza place has a two-hour wait, and because pad see ew sounds like comfort food. While we wait, Sawyer flips through channels until he lands on some action movie

—explosions and car chases that feel absurdly tame compared to our last forty-eight hours.

"The physics are all wrong," he mutters during a particularly ridiculous crash sequence.

"You're critiquing the realism of a movie where the hero just jumped a motorcycle onto a helicopter."

"Still. Basic physics should apply."

I laugh, and it feels strange. Normal. Like we're just two people spending a lazy afternoon together instead of two people who might not survive the week.

The food arrives, and we eat cross-legged on the bed, containers spread between us. He steals bites from mine even though he ordered the same thing. I pretend to be annoyed. He grins like he knows I'm not.

"When this is over," I say, then stop. Because I don't know how to finish that sentence, *when this is over,* assumes we both make it out. Assumes there's an *after.*

"When this is over," Sawyer says quietly, "I'm taking you somewhere normal. Dinner. A movie. Maybe dancing if you're into that."

"I'm a terrible dancer."

"Good. So am I."

The movie plays on, forgotten. His hand finds mine, fingers lacing together, and I'm struck by how easy this is. How *right* it feels to be here with him, despite everything.

Despite the fact that I've known him less than three days. Despite the fact that we're both probably going to die.

I should be terrified. I *am* terrified. But not of dying—of losing this. This feeling like I've finally found something I didn't know I was looking for.

"Come here," he murmurs, pulling me closer.

We make love again, slower this time. Less desperate. His hands map every inch of my skin like he's memorizing me. I let myself get lost in him, in us, in this perfect impossible moment that feels stolen from someone else's life.

Afterward, he holds me against his chest, heartbeat steady under my ear. I trace the scars on his ribs—the ones I noticed earlier but didn't ask about.

"Bosnia," he says quietly. "Shrapnel."

"The burns?"

"Different deployment. Different bad day."

I kiss the scarred skin. He pulls me tighter.

The movie has ended. Another one starts—something with subtitles that neither of us read. Outside, the sun sets, painting the room in shades of amber and gold. It's beautiful and surreal and terrifying because I know this ends. Tomorrow, or the day after, this bubble bursts, and we're back in the real world where people are trying to kill me.

Where I might lose him.

Where he might lose me.

"What are you thinking?" His voice is rough with exhaustion.

"That this doesn't feel real."

"It's real."

"I've known you three days."

"Yeah." His hand slides into my hair. "Feels longer, doesn't it?"

It does. It feels like I've known him forever and no time at all. Like we're running out of time even as we have all the time in the world.

"I'm scared," I whisper.

"Me too."

"Of dying?"

"Of losing you."

My throat tightens. I don't trust myself to speak, so I just hold him tighter, memorizing the feel of him. The weight of his arms around me. The way his breathing slows as he starts to drift off.

I should sleep. I know I should. But I'm afraid that if I close my eyes, this disappears. That I'll wake up and find out it was all a dream, or worse—that I'll wake up alone.

Eventually, exhaustion wins. I sink into sleep wrapped in him, his heartbeat the last thing I'm aware of.

Safe. For now.

I wake to Sawyer's phone buzzing. He's wrapped around me,

skin to skin, and for a moment I let myself pretend this is normal. That we're normal people who met normally and have a normal future ahead.

"Yeah," he answers, voice rough with sleep. "Copy that. ETA?"

Reality crashes back. The mission. Prometheus. Mass murder.

"Teams are thirty minutes out," he tells me, already moving. "We need to get ready."

The loss of his warmth makes me shiver. I watch him dress, cataloging new details—a scar on his lower back I hadn't seen before, the way he automatically checks his weapon even half-asleep, how he looks younger in the pre-dawn light.

"Stop staring and get dressed," he says without turning around.

"How did you—"

"I can feel you thinking." He turns, and his expression is soft. "No regrets?"

"None. You?"

"Only that we don't have more time."

I head to the bathroom, take a quick shower, and dress quickly.

A knock interrupts—three short, two long, one short. Code.

"That's them." Sawyer checks the peephole, then opens the door.

Two men enter, and the room immediately feels smaller. The first is massive—shoulders that barely fit through the doorway. The second is leaner but no less dangerous, with dark hair and scars that make Sawyer's look mild.

"Name's Flint," the blond one says, offering me a hand that could crush mine without effort. "Heard you've been giving Hawk here a run for his money."

The other one takes in the room, the rumpled bed, then turns to Sawyer. "You're supposed to be running a simple extraction. Now, you've got us assaulting Titan International." He turns to me and offers a hand. "Colt. Nice to meet you."

"Gentlemen." Another voice from the doorway, a man with the bearing of someone used to command. "Ms. Cross. I'm CJ, Lead for the Guardian teams. Flint and Frost are feral."

"Frost?" I look between the men.

"That's me." Colt lifts his hand.

Unlike Colt—Frost—who checked out the room, CJ focuses solely on me. Cataloging threats, skills, and potential. Then he nods. "Hawk says you have intel on Prometheus."

Hawk?

Ah, like Frost, that must be Sawyer's nickname. Or is it a call sign? I shake my head.

"Yes. Everything." I open my shiny new laptop. "Membership lists, chemical compositions, target locations, timeline. Nathan encrypted it, but I've broken most of it."

"Our tech team can handle the rest," CJ says.

"What?" I look to Sawyer, then back to CJ. "No. I've been inside Nathan's head for three years. I know how he thinks, how he codes. Your tech team will be fumbling in the dark."

"Our tech team has cleared NSA-level encryption." CJ's tone doesn't change. "They can handle it."

"Not in the time frame you have." I pull up the file structure. "See this? Nathan used a cascading cipher system that references classical literature. Your team could crack it eventually, but I can do it in hours because I know which books he was reading."

CJ's eyes narrow slightly. First point to me.

"Fine. You work with our analysts and brief the tech team."

"And I'm going in the field."

"Negative."

"I can shoot, I can fight." I meet his gaze head-on. "You need me."

"What I need is an operator who won't get my men killed." CJ crosses his arms. "Convince me you're an asset in the field, not a liability."

"I've survived three days with them hunting me. I built a dead man's switch and stayed alive long enough for Sawyer to extract me. I don't need to justify myself to you—I'm offering a partnership."

Frost whistles low. "Hawk, you sure can pick them. She's got spunk."

"Spunk doesn't mean training," CJ says. "Our teams are highly skilled and integrated. They work as a unit. This isn't the time or place to insert yourself into that dynamic."

"Then put me on comms. Tactical support." I'm not backing down. "I can warn your teams before they walk into something your intel doesn't cover."

There's a beat of silence.

"She's not wrong." Sawyer's voice is quiet but carries weight.

CJ's jaw tightens. "You're vouching for her?"

"I've seen her in action with trained operators hunting her. That counts for something."

CJ studies me for a long moment. "Tactical support only. You stay with comms. The second you become a liability, you're out. Clear?"

It's not boots on the ground, but it's not sitting in some safe house either. "Clear."

"Good. Ms. Cross, you have thirty minutes to brief our tech team, then you're with me." He turns to Hawk. "Alpha and Bravo are in this. Your team's not fully kitted out, but I'm sure, between the three of you, you can show up for Echo team.

He turns to leave, and I catch Sawyer's eye. There's something there—approval, maybe concern. He gives me a slight nod.

I got my foot in the door. Now I have to prove I belong there.

ELEVEN

Sawyer

THE TITAN INTERNATIONAL LOGISTICS HUB SQUATS AGAINST THE LA skyline like a cancer—twelve acres of warehouses, chemical storage, and loading bays surrounded by razor wire and cameras. From our position on the adjacent building, guards patrol in predictable patterns through my night vision scope. Competent but complacent.

They think they're guarding industrial chemicals, not weapons of mass destruction.

They're wrong.

"Two-minute intervals between patrols on the north side," Frost murmurs beside me, his voice barely audible through the comms. "Cameras have a three-second lag when they pivot. Doable."

Colt "Frost" Harrison—once Syria, once Colombia, a hundred ops in between. The man's a ghost when he needs to be, cold and deadly efficient.

"Thermal's showing three roving patrols inside," Flint adds from my other side, studying his handheld scanner. "Two static positions at the loading docks. They're clustered—suggests they're guarding something specific."

Jake "Flint" Morrison. Former Delta, breacher extraordinaire, and the kind of operator who can read a building's defensive setup like most people read a menu. Between him and Frost, we've run enough missions to move like parts of the same weapon.

"Alpha team in position," Max's voice crackles through my earpiece. "North entrance is clear."

"Bravo team ready at the south gate," Brady confirms. "On your signal, Hawk."

0158 on my watch. At noon, Prometheus plans to dump enough poison into LA's water supply to kill tens of thousands. The chemicals sit below us, ready for distribution. We stop them tonight, or we don't stop them at all.

"Remember," CJ's voice comes through from the mobile command center, "Savannah needs to access their mainframe to identify which chemicals are prepped and where they're staged. Without that intel, we could blow the whole place and still miss the active compounds."

Savannah checks her equipment beside me, kitted out in tactical gear that would look like dress-up on someone else. But her eyes—focused, determined, ready—tell a different story. The Glock on her hip isn't for show.

"You sure about this?" One more time.

"The mainframe requires biometric access," she says, checking her magazine. "Nathan programmed it to recognize select Prometheus members. What he didn't know is that I cloned his biometric signature months ago when I suspected he was hiding something." She holds up a device that looks like a thick smartphone. "I can trick the system, but I have to be physically present."

Solid reason. Doesn't mean I like it.

"Stay between Frost and me at all times," I tell her. "If shooting starts—"

"I drop and find cover while you handle threats." She meets my eyes. "This isn't my first firefight, remember?"

No, it's not. But that doesn't stop the protective instinct that makes me want to lock her in the command vehicle and handle this without her.

"Hawk." Frost's hand on my shoulder. "She's tougher than she looks. Trust her."

Flint nods once, a silent agreement. The man doesn't waste words when a look will do.

Tyler trusted me, and that didn't save him.

"All teams, we go on my mark," I say into comms. "Rules of engagement—anyone armed is hostile. We need the server room intact; everything else is expendable. Priority is destroying the chemicals staged for tomorrow's attack."

"Copy," comes from multiple voices.

Savannah chambers a round in her Glock, the sound sharp in the darkness. "Let's burn their world down."

"Mark."

We move.

Frost and Flint go first on the rappel lines, fast and silent, hitting the ground together. Immediately, they split—Frost left, Flint right —creating a security diamond. The movement is instinctive, practiced. They don't need to communicate it.

Savannah and I follow, my arm around her waist, controlling our descent. She doesn't shake this time—three days of being hunted has burned the fear out of her, replaced it with purpose.

"North breach," Max reports, followed by the muffled thump of a breaching charge.

"South breach," Brady confirms.

Gunfire erupts from both directions—the guards responding faster than expected. Professional security, not mall cops. Alpha and Bravo teams draw them off, giving our smaller team time to infiltrate.

"Moving to secondary," I tell them, leading toward the service entrance Intel identified.

The lock is electronic, high-end. Savannah steps forward with her device, fingers flying across the screen. Frost and I take positions on either side of the door, weapons up. Flint takes three steps back, scanning our six with thermal.

"Thirty seconds," she says.

Movement to our left—a guard coming around the corner. Frost's weapon tracks, and the guard drops with a suppressed double-tap before he can radio for help.

Professional. Clean.

"Thermal's clear for twenty meters," Flint murmurs. "But we've got heat signatures converging from the east wing. Two minutes, maybe three."

"In," Savannah says as the lock disengages.

The service corridor is industrial plain—concrete floors, exposed pipes, fluorescent lighting that makes everything look sick. Building plans showed the server room in sublevel 2, northeast corner. Four minutes if we meet no resistance.

Ninety seconds in, we meet resistance.

Three guards in tactical formation come up from the stairwell. They open fire immediately.

"Down!" I shove Savannah behind a support pillar as rounds spark off concrete.

Frost moves right without a word. Flint breaks left. The three of us create overlapping fields of fire—wordless coordination born from a hundred missions. Frost's suppressed weapon coughs twice. One guard drops. Flint's rifle barks, and the second crumples. The third tries to retreat.

Two rounds in his back before he reaches the door.

"Clear," Frost calls.

"Clear," from Flint.

Savannah's already moving from cover, weapon up, eyes scanning like we taught her. Good instincts.

"Alpha encountering heavy resistance," Max reports. "They were ready for us."

My blood goes cold. "It's a trap?"

"Unknown. Pushing through."

We take the stairs fast, Savannah between us. Frost leads, Flint takes rear security, and I stay on Savannah—a moving triangle formation that keeps her protected while maintaining 360-degree coverage. We don't discuss it.

We just move.

Sublevel 2 is darker, emergency lighting only. The server room door requires another hack, and while Savannah works, Frost and I create a defensive position. Flint moves ten feet back, thermal scanner active, reading the corridor behind us.

"Multiple heat signatures approaching from above," Flint says quietly. "They know we're here."

That's when Nathan Torres steps out of the shadows, FBI credentials visible, weapon holstered.

"Hello, Savi."

Savannah goes rigid beside me, her weapon coming up, but Nathan raises his hands.

"I'm not here to fight," Nathan says, eyes locked on Savannah. "I'm here to offer you a deal."

"The only deal you're getting is life in prison instead of a needle." My Glock centers on his chest.

He doesn't look at me. "Savi, you don't understand what you're doing. The system is broken. We're trying to fix it."

"By murdering thousands of innocent people?" Her voice is steady, but the tremor runs through her where our shoulders touch.

"Casualties of war. Every revolution requires sacrifice."

"Titan security converging on your position," CJ warns through comms. "Whatever you're doing, do it fast."

Nathan steps closer. I shift to maintain my shot angle. Frost adjusts left without being asked, creating a crossfire. Flint hasn't moved from his position, but his rifle tracks Nathan's center mass. Three weapons, three operators, one target.

"Walk away, Savi. Take your friends and disappear. We'll let you go."

"Like you let those FBI agents go?" She circles slightly. "You killed three good people."

"Symbols of a corrupt system." His facade cracks, showing the fanatic underneath. "Just like I'll kill anyone who stands in our way."

His hand lifts toward his jacket.

"Gun!" I shout, but Savannah's already moving.

She shoots him twice—center mass—before his weapon clears the holster. Nathan staggers, looking more surprised than hurt, body armor visible through the holes in his shirt.

"You shot me." Genuine shock. "You actually—"

Frost puts the third round through his forehead, dropping him instantly.

"Deadman switch," Frost says calmly, kicking a device away from Nathan's corpse. "Would have triggered explosives throughout the facility."

Savannah stares at Nathan's body for a heartbeat, then turns away. "The server room. We need to move."

No breakdown, no tears. She compartmentalizes like a professional.

The server room door yields to her device, and we're in—rows of humming servers, multiple terminals, the digital heart of Titan's operation.

"Two minutes," she says, plugging in her equipment. "I need to find the chemical manifests and distribution protocols."

"Bravo team, we need those trucks disabled," I call through comms.

"On it," Brady responds. "Count eight vehicles in the loading bay."

Gunfire echoes from above—Alpha team still engaged. Through the reinforced windows, security forces mass in the warehouse proper.

Flint takes position at the door, rifle braced. "They're stacking up out there. Preparing for dynamic entry."

Frost moves to the opposite corner, creating a crossfire angle. "Estimate twenty hostiles. They'll breach in under a minute."

The two of them work like mirror images—Frost checking his magazines, Flint adjusting his position slightly for better coverage. No wasted movement. No unnecessary communication.

"Got it." Savannah's eyes race across screens of data. "They're using chlorine trifluoride as the base—it reacts violently with water, creating hydrogen fluoride gas. But they've stabilized it with... Jesus. With compounds that delay the reaction by twelve hours. By the time symptoms appear, thousands will have consumed it."

"Can we neutralize it?"

"Not here, not without proper equipment. But—" Her fingers fly across keys. "The distribution system requires specific pressure and temperature controls. If I corrupt the delivery protocols, the chemicals become inert before they reach the water supply."

"Do it."

She works with fierce concentration. Frost and Flint hold the door, weapons trained on the entry point. Laser dots dance under the door frame—multiple shooters, lined up for breach.

"Forty seconds," Savannah says.

"They're moving," Flint reports, calm as discussing the weather. "Breaching team in position."

"Alpha team, we need a distraction," I call.

"Little busy," Max grunts, gunfire heavy over his transmission.

The door explodes inward.

Training takes over. I push Savannah down, covering her with my body. Frost and Flint engage simultaneously—controlled pairs, perfect rhythm. Frost drops two hostiles in the fatal funnel. Flint takes out the breacher. The space fills with gunfire, concrete dust, and screaming ricochets.

"Reloading," Frost calls.

"Covering," Flint responds instantly, increasing his rate of fire to suppress the entry point while Frost swaps magazines. Three seconds later, they reverse—Flint reloading, Frost covering.

Like breathing.

"Almost there." Savannah keeps typing beneath me, even with bullets sparking off the server housing inches from her head.

Frost takes a round in the shoulder, spins, but keeps shooting. We're being overrun—too many hostiles, not enough cover.

This is it. This is the moment. Tyler's death replays in my mind —the hesitation, being three seconds too late, watching fire consume him.

Not again. Not her.

"FROST! FLINT! DEMO CHARGES!"

They get it immediately. Flint pulls C4 from his pack. Not to blow the chemicals—that would be catastrophic—but the ceiling. Bring it down, create a barrier.

But it'll trap us in here.

"Done!" Savannah shouts. "Protocols corrupted, distribution system locked out."

"Move!"

I haul her up, and we run for the secondary exit. Flint triggers the charges, the explosion deafening. The ceiling comes down in a cascade of concrete and rebar. But the debris doesn't fall evenly—a massive chunk breaks free directly above Savannah.

Time slows.

Three seconds. That's what I had with Tyler. Three seconds to act or watch someone die.

I don't hesitate.

I hit Savannah with my full body weight, driving her clear as the concrete crashes down. My left leg doesn't make it—the edge of the debris catches it, crushing weight that snaps bone and tears muscle.

The pain is immediate and absolute, but she's alive. She's alive, and that's all that matters.

"SAWYER!" She scrambles back to me, hands on my face, my chest, checking for damage.

"Get out," I grit through the pain. "Frost, Flint, get her out."

"Not leaving you." She's crying now, trying to lift the concrete. "I'm not letting you die for me."

"Building's coming down." Brady's voice through comms. "All teams evac now."

Frost and Flint are already moving—Frost with a pry bar on the debris, Flint pulling a second bar from his pack. They work to leverage the weight while Savannah pulls at my vest. The concrete shifts enough—barely enough—and they drag me free. My leg is mangled, useless, blood pooling fast.

"Move, move, move."

Frost takes one arm, Flint the other, and they carry me between them. Every step is agony, every jostle threatens to black me out. But Savannah's voice keeps me conscious—fierce, determined, refusing to let me go.

We burst out of the building as explosions rip through it—not the chemicals, but the infrastructure. Trucks are burning, and distribution systems are destroyed. Prometheus's attack dies in a blaze of flame and twisted metal.

"Medic!" Savannah screams as we clear the perimeter.

Flint's already on the radio. "Guardian Actual, Hawk is down. Severe leg trauma, significant blood loss. Need immediate evac."

The team medics converge. They assess my injuries instantly—tourniquets, pressure bandages, IV lines. But I only see Savannah's face—dirty, tear-streaked, beautiful, and alive.

"You saved me," she says, gripping my hand as they work. "You didn't hesitate."

"Told you," I manage through gritted teeth. "Nothing bad happens to you on my watch."

"You stupid, noble bastard." She kisses me hard, not caring about the blood or the audience. "If you die on me, I'll kill you."

"Not dying." The drugs they're pushing make everything fuzzy, but I need her to know. "Tyler would be proud. Saved the girl."

"Yeah," Flint says from somewhere above me, his voice unusually gentle. "You saved the girl, brother. Mission accomplished."

Frost's hand grips my shoulder—brief, firm. Brotherhood distilled into a single gesture.

As consciousness fades, sirens wail in the distance—medical, fire, police. The chemicals are secured, Prometheus is finished, and Savannah is alive. The weight I've carried for years—Tyler's death, my hesitation, my failure—finally lifts.

This time, I was enough.

TWELVE

Savannah

The FBI debriefing room smells like burnt coffee and bureaucracy, fluorescent lights harsh after three hours of questions.

Maria Santos sits across from me, recording device between us, going through every detail for the fifth time. Sawyer's in medical, getting his leg properly treated—the field dressing held through the fight, but he needs real surgery to repair the damage.

"Walk me through the code sequence again," Santos says, patient but thorough.

I explain, again, how Nathan built his redundancies, where he made mistakes, and how I recognized his coding signature. My throat aches where he choked me, voice rough, but I keep talking. This testimony will put away what's left of Prometheus, and I want them buried.

"The chemical formula he was using," Santos continues. "Where did he source the knowledge?"

"He had access to classified studies on water treatment vulnerabilities from his time consulting for Homeland Security." I pull up the files on my laptop. "Here. Every study they accessed, every weakness they exploited."

Santos reviews the data, and her expression grows grimmer. "This could have worked. If you hadn't stopped them—"

"We did stop them." I'm too tired for hypotheticals.

"Yes." She closes the file. "Which brings me to it. The FBI wants you back. Full reinstatement, your choice of assignments, commendation for stopping a terrorist attack."

Four days ago, I would have accepted immediately. The FBI was my life, my purpose, my identity. Now...

"I need time to think."

Santos's eyebrows rise. "Time? We're offering complete vindication."

"I understand. But I almost died for an organization that turned on me the moment Nathan pointed a finger." I meet her eyes. "I need to decide if I can trust the system again."

"The system failed you. But you could help fix it from the inside."

"Maybe. Or maybe I can do more good from outside." I stand, and exhaustion makes the room tilt slightly. "I'll give you an answer tomorrow."

"Savannah—" She pauses, seems to really see me for the first time. "You're different. This experience changed you."

"It showed me who I really am." I manage a tired smile. "Turns out I'm not just an analyst who follows rules."

I leave before she can respond and leave for the hospital. Sawyer's in recovery, and the nurse tries to stop me from entering.

"Family only—"

"I'm his fiancée." The lie comes easily, but the ring of truth in it surprises me.

She lets me pass.

Sawyer's awake, right leg pinned and immobilized, but looking better than he has in hours. His eyes find mine immediately.

"Hey, troublemaker."

"Hey yourself." I take the chair beside his bed, our default position now. "How's the leg?"

"Repairable. Two surgeries, six weeks of physical therapy, but full recovery expected." He reaches for my hand with his left. "How was the debrief?"

"Thorough. Santos offered me reinstatement."

His expression is carefully neutral. "That's good. It's what you wanted."

"It's what I thought I wanted." I trace patterns on his palm. "But that was before."

"Before what?"

"Before I met someone worth changing everything for."

His fingers tighten on mine. "Savannah—"

"CJ offered me a position. Field cyber warfare specialist. I'd work with the Guardian teams, help prevent situations like Prometheus." I meet his eyes.

"You can't make career decisions based on—"

"On the man who saved my life repeatedly? On the person I trust most in the world? On someone I'm pretty sure I'm falling in love with?" I lean closer. "Watch me."

He pulls me down, kisses me with days of suppressed want. When we break apart, we're both breathing hard.

"I love you too," he says against my mouth. "In case that wasn't clear."

"You barely know me."

"I know you turn earrings into weapons. I know you face your fears even when terrified. I know you dragged me bleeding out of Titan's facility and never let go." His thumb brushes my cheekbone. "I know enough."

"This is insane. It's too fast."

"Probably."

"We're bonded by trauma.."

"Definitely."

"It might not work without the adrenaline."

"Only one way to find out." He kisses me again, gentler this time. "Take the job. Move here. Let's see what we are when no one's shooting at us."

"What if we're boring without death threats?"

"Then we'll be boring together."

I laugh, my first real laugh in days. "Okay."

"Okay?"

"Okay, I'll take the job. Okay, I'll move here. Okay, I'll see where this goes." I kiss his forehead, his cheeks, his mouth. "Okay, I love you too, you beautiful disaster."

"That's my line."

The nurse returns and insists that visiting hours are over. I promise to return in the morning, but Sawyer doesn't let go of my hand.

"Stay."

"I can't—hospital rules—"

"I've been shot, blown up, and saved California from a chemical incident. They can bend the rules."

The nurse looks between us, sighs. "Fine. But if anyone asks, she snuck in after my shift ended."

She leaves, and I curl up in the chair that's become my second home. Sawyer's hand finds mine again.

"Tell me about after," I say. "When you're healed, and I'm settled, and life is normal. What does that look like?"

"Sunday mornings without alarms. Coffee that doesn't taste like dirt. Teaching you to rock climb and rappel properly so you're not terrified of heights."

"I'll always be terrified of heights."

"But you'll climb anyway. Because you're brave like that." His voice goes softer. "Maybe a house near the beach. You said you love beaches."

"I do."

"Dinner with my team. You'll love them—they're all slightly insane, just like us."

"Sounds perfect."

"Yeah?"

"Yeah."

He falls asleep holding my hand, and I watch him breathe, this man who jumped out a window for a stranger. My phone buzzes— text from CJ at Guardian HRS, inquiring about the position. I accept without hesitation.

The next morning brings chaos—media attention, official statements, and enough paperwork to build a fort. But through it all, Sawyer and I stay connected, orbiting each other even when pulled in different directions.

I feel nothing over Nathan's death—no satisfaction, no regret, just hollow acknowledgment that it's over.

By evening, I'm officially no longer FBI. My credentials surrendered, my access revoked, my five-year career ended with a form and a handshake. Santos hugs me, tells me I'll always have a place if I change my mind. I thank her, but I won't be back.

Guardian HRS sends a car, and I arrive at their facility as the sun sets over the mountains. CJ himself does the tour, showing me the technical division where I'll work. State-of-the-art everything, quantum computing access, and a team that looks at me with respect instead of suspicion.

He hands me a tablet with my first assignment. "Titan is rebuilding their chemical division. Want to make sure they can't?"

"Absolutely."

"Then welcome to Guardian HRS, Ms. Cross."

Sawyer's waiting when the tour ends, leg in a brace but mobile. "How'd it go?"

"I start Monday."

"That's four days away."

"Recovery time, apparently. CJ insists I need to sleep for seventy-two hours before tackling Titan."

"Sounds about right." He's dressed in jeans and a Henley that does wonderful things to his chest. "Have dinner with me."

"Now?"

"Now. No running, no shooting, no bombs. Just food and conversation and seeing if we work without adrenaline."

"What if we don't?"

"Then we'll manufacture some adrenaline." His grin is wicked. "I have ideas."

"I bet you do."

Dinner is a tiny Italian place where the owner knows Sawyer by name and insists we take the corner booth reserved for special occasions. We eat too much, drink wine that makes me warm, and talk about everything except the last few days.

I learn he rebuilds motorcycles when he can't sleep. He learns I play violin badly but enthusiastically. I discover he reads poetry, secretly. He discovers I've never seen a Star Wars movie, which apparently is a crime against humanity.

"We'll have to fix that," he says, scandalized.

"We'll have to fix a lot of things." I trace the rim of my wine glass. "I don't know how to do normal, Sawyer. Five years of being an analyst, three days of being... whatever I am now."

"You're yourself. Just more honest about it."

"Is that enough?"

He reaches across the table and takes my hand. "You're enough exactly as you are."

"You're just saying that because I saved your life."

"I'm saying it because it's true. The life-saving was just a bonus."

We walk back to his apartment—he insists on showing me the neighborhood since I'll be living here. His place is exactly what I expected—clean, organized, with minimal decoration, except for photos of his team and Tyler's challenge coin, now displayed proudly on a shelf.

"Guest room's yours as long as you need it," he says, suddenly formal.

"Guest room?"

"I didn't want to assume—"

I kiss him, cutting off whatever noble thing he was about to say. "I don't want the guest room."

"Savannah—"

"We've been through hell together. We've saved each other's lives. We've said we love each other." I frame his face with my hands. "I don't want to sleep alone tonight. Or tomorrow. Or any night if I have a choice."

"My leg—"

"We'll be creative."

He laughs, dark and appreciative. "You're going to be trouble, aren't you?"

"The best kind."

We're creative.

Careful of injuries but not of feelings.

He maps my body like he's memorizing terrain, and I discover scars he didn't mention, each with a story he whispers against my skin. When release finds us, it's with my name on his lips and his on mine, a promise and a claim and a beginning all at once.

After, tangled carefully around bandages and bruises, I trace lazy patterns on his chest.

"No regrets?" he asks.

"None. Is this what normal looks like for us?"

"Probably." He presses a kiss to my hair. "That okay?"

"Perfect."

I fall asleep to his heartbeat, steady and sure, the rhythm that kept me going when everything else fell apart. Tomorrow there'll be paperwork, arrangements, and the business of building a new life. But tonight, there's just this—us, together, alive despite the odds.

When I wake at 3 AM from habit and trauma, he's awake too, watching the ceiling. Without words, I curl closer, and his arm comes around me, anchoring us both.

"Can't sleep?"

"No."

"Want to talk about it?"

"Not yet."

"Okay."

We lie in comfortable silence, two damaged people choosing to heal together.

It shouldn't work. It's too fast, too intense, built on a foundation of violence and fear. But maybe that's why it does work—we've seen each other at our worst and chose to stay anyway.

"I love you," I say into the darkness.

"I love you too."

Simple words for a complicated truth, but they're enough. We're enough.

Together.

THIRTEEN

Epilogue

SAVANNAH

Six Months Later

"You're still dropping your shoulder on the left cross."

I adjust my stance in the Guardian HRS gym, sweat dripping. Sawyer circles me, critical eye catching every flaw in my form. His leg is fully healed, barely a scar remaining, and he moves with the lethal prowress that caught my attention that first night when he saved me.

"Better?" I throw the combination again.

"Better. But your footwork's sloppy."

"Your teaching's sloppy."

He grins, steps into my space. "Insult the teacher, pay the price."

I duck his playful grab, use his momentum against him—a move he taught me—and somehow we end up against the wall, me pinning him despite the weight difference. His eyes darken, and the air between us charges the way it always does.

"Gym's for training," CJ's voice cuts through the moment. "Not whatever this is."

We spring apart like guilty teenagers. CJ stands at parade rest, amused despite his stern tone.

"Morning briefing in five," he tells us. "New situation in Seattle. Domestic terror cell. Cross, I need your expertise."

"On it."

CJ leaves, and Sawyer pulls me back for a quick kiss. "Be careful up there."

"You're not coming?"

"Different assignment. Close protection for a federal judge getting death threats." He traces my cheek. "First time we've been separated since you started."

"We'll manage."

"We will." But his arms tighten around me. "Come home safe."

"You too."

The Seattle operation takes four days. Four days of decryption, analysis, and ultimately preventing another Prometheus-style attack before it starts.

I work with a different Guardian team. When it's over, seventeen arrests are made with no casualties. I understand why Sawyer loves this work. It's not just the adrenaline. It's knowing you made a difference.

I arrive home—his apartment has become home without discussion—at midnight on the fourth day. Sawyer's waiting, takeout from our Italian place already plated, wine breathing on the counter.

"How'd you know when I'd be back?"

"Tracked your flight." He pulls me close, breathes me in. "Missed you."

"Missed you too."

We eat, sharing stories of our respective missions, the domesticity of it striking me. Three months ago, I was alone, trusting no one. Now I'm debriefing over pasta with a man who knows exactly how I like my wine and keeps my preferred coffee in three locations throughout the apartment.

Later, in bed, I trace the newest scar on his collection—a graze from the judge's would-be assassin. "We live dangerous lives."

"We do."

"Either of us could die on any mission."

"We could."

"Doesn't that scare you?"

He rolls to face me fully. "What scares me is wasting time we have being afraid of time we might not get."

"Philosophy again?"

"Life experience." He kisses my forehead. "Every day with you is a gift. I'm not going to waste them worrying about when they might end."

"Even if it ends tomorrow?"

"Especially then."

I curl into him, this man who chose me over his own safety again and again. "I love you."

"I love you too."

My phone buzzes—emergency alert from Guardian HRS. Another crisis, another threat, another chance to save lives. Sawyer's phone buzzes, too.

Same alert.

We look at each other, already reaching for clothes.

"Together?" he asks.

"Together."

AUTHOR'S NOTE:
Thank you for reading HAWK!

IF YOU'RE CRAVING MORE HIGH-STAKES MISSIONS, MORALLY GRAY operators, and romance forged in gunfire—I've got you covered.

DESIRE ANOTHER GUARDIAN HRS SHORT READ? KADE IS NEXT. You can read it HERE.

· · ·

BINGE THE GUARDIAN HOSTAGE RESCUE SPECIALISTS (HRS) WORLD NOW

THE GUARDIAN HRS UNIVERSE IS MASSIVE, AND MULTIPLE complete series are waiting for you:

🔥 **GUARDIAN HRS CORE SERIES** - *COMPLETE AND READY to binge* **Alpha, Bravo, Charlie,** and **Delta** teams handling the extractions governments won't touch. These operators live in the shadows, fight in the dark, and fall hard for the women who make them want to step into the light.
- Elite hostage rescue specialists
- International black ops missions
- Brothers-in-arms who become family
- The women tough enough to love them

START WITH ALPHA TEAM, BOOK 1 → RESCUING ZOE → READ HERE

CERBERUS PERSONAL SECURITY SERIES -*GHOST, BRASS,* and **Whisper,** *with more coming soon.*

THE **CERBERUS** SERIES IS GUARDIAN HRS ADJACENT - **Grittier, Darker, More Possessive**

When Guardian HRS needs someone protected but the threat level is DEFCON 1, they call Cerberus. These aren't your typical bodyguards—they're the operators who live between protection and elimination. More alpha. More possessive. More willing to cross lines the Guardians won't.

Think: Dominant protector heroes who'll burn the world down to keep their woman safe.

• Close protection with deadly force authorized

• Operators who don't play by the rules

• Obsessive, possessive, "mine to protect" romance

• Higher heat, darker themes

Start with GHOST → READ HERE

Can't decide? Want it all?

→ Read Guardian HRS first (it's the foundation), then dive into Cerberus for the grittier adjacent operations.

THE GUARDIAN HRS PROMISE:

Every book features:

☑ Competent, dangerous heroes with hidden depths

☑ Strong heroines who don't need saving (but get protected anyway)

☑ Found family and brotherhood

☑ Realistic tactical operations (I do my research)

☑ Romance that earns the HEA

☑ Standalone books with interconnected world

DON'T WAIT - START YOUR BINGE NOW

A PERSONAL INVITATION

Colt and Maggie's story is a 25,000 word **NOVELLA**—just a taste and a quick, intense introduction to the Guardian HRS world. But here's what you need to know: **nearly every other book in this universe is a massive, extra-long novel.**

We're talking 80,000-100,000+ words of:
- Complex multi-layered missions
- Deep character development
- Multiple POVs and subplots
- Extended tactical operations
- Slow-burn romance that EARNS the payoff
- Brotherhood dynamics and found family

FROST gave you a taste. The full series gives you a FEAST.

Think of this novella as your amuse-bouche—a carefully crafted bite designed to show you what I'm capable of.

. . .

THE MAIN GUARDIAN HRS AND CERBERUS BOOKS? THOSE ARE five-course meals. Beefy, satisfying, the kind of novels you lose an entire weekend to because you physically cannot put them down.

IF COLT AND MAGGIE'S STORY RESONATED WITH YOU IN JUST 25,000 words—if you felt Colt's guilt, Maggie's betrayal, and the desperate need for something REAL in a world of lies—imagine what I can do with **four times the page count.**

THE FULL-LENGTH NOVELS DIVE DEEP:
- Operators with complex trauma and layered backstories
- Missions that span multiple countries and weeks of operations
- Romance that develops over hundreds of pages (not hours)
- Secondary characters who become your new obsessions
- Plot twists that will make you gasp at 2 AM
- Action sequences that feel like watching a movie

The Guardian HRS world is waiting.
Your next operator is loading his weapon.
And you've got 30+ extra-long novels ready to devour.

WHICH TEAM WILL YOU CHOOSE?

STAY DANGEROUS,

Ellie Masters

🔥 START BINGING NOW 🔥

Guardian HRS Alpha Team, Book 1: RESCUING ZOE →
CLICK HERE

Cerberus Book 1: GHOST → CLICK HERE

The Guardian HRS world has **30+** complete books waiting for you. Operators are falling in love. Missions are launching. And somewhere in this universe, your next *book boyfriend* is loading his weapon and preparing to risk everything for the woman who makes him feel human again.

🎯 READY FOR YOUR NEXT MISSION?

ELLZ BELLZ

ELLIE'S FACEBOOK READER GROUP

If you are interested in joining the ELLZ BELLZ, Ellie's Facebook reader group, we'd love to have you.

Join Ellie's ELLZ BELLZ.
The ELLZ BELLZ Facebook Reader Group

Sign up for Ellie's Newsletter.
Elliemasters.com/newslettersignup

Also by Ellie Masters

The LIGHTER SIDE

Ellie Masters is the lighter side of the Jet & Ellie Masters writing duo! You will find Contemporary Romance, Military Romance, Romantic Suspense, Billionaire Romance, and Rock Star Romance in Ellie's Works.

YOU CAN FIND ELLIE'S BOOKS HERE:

ELLIEMASTERS.COM/BOOKS

Shop Ellie Masters Romantic Suspense and Steamy Contemporary Romance by series.

Angel Fire Rock Romance

Guardian HRS: Alpha Team

Guardian HRS: Bravo Team

Guardian HRS: Charlie Team

Guardian HRS: Delta Team

Cerberus Personal Security

The LaRouge Triplets

The One I Want Series

Angel's Peak Series

Billionaire Boy's Club

The Lovers

Changing Roles

SUGGESTED READING ORDER

START HERE

Rockstar Romance

The Angel Fire Rock Romance Series

EACH BOOK IN THIS SERIES CAN BE READ AS A STANDALONE AND IS ABOUT A DIFFERENT COUPLE WITH AN HEA.

IT IS RECOMMENDED THEY ARE READ IN ORDER.

Heart's Insanity

Ashes to New

Heart's Desire

Heart's Collide

Hearts Divided

Hearts Entwined

Forest's FALL

Hearts The Last Beat

CONTINUE HERE...

Military Romance

Guardian Hostage Rescue Specialists

Rescuing Melissa

(Get a FREE copy of Rescuing Melissa

when you join Ellie's Newsletter)

Alpha Team

Rescuing Zoe

Rescuing Moira

Rescuing Eve

Rescuing Lily

Rescuing Jinx

Rescuing Maria

Bravo Team

Rescuing Angie

Rescuing Isabelle

Rescuing Carmen

Rescuing Rosalie

Rescuing Kaye

Cara's Protector

Rescuing Barbi

Charlie Team

Rescuing Rebel

Rescuing Stitch

Rescuing Mia

Jenna's Protector

Rescuing Sophia

Rescuing Malia

Rescuing Ally (Part 1)

Rescuing Ally (Part 2)

Delta Team

Rescuing Ember

Rescuing Aria

STANDALONES IN THE GUARDIAN HOSTAGE RESCUE SERIES YOU CAN READ ANYTIME

Military Romance

Guardian Personal Protection Specialists

Sybil's Protector

Lyra's Protector

Angel's Peak Series

Steamy Instalove Small Town

Brody

Cage

Billionaire Romance

Billionaire Boys Club

Hawke

Richard

Contemporary Romance

Cocky Captain

Romantic Suspense

EACH BOOK IS A STANDALONE NOVEL.

The Starling

The Swan

~AND~

Science Fiction

Ellie Masters writing as L.A. Warren

Vendel Rising: a Science Fiction Serialized Novel

If you enjoyed this book by Ellie Masters, the LIGHTER SIDE of the Jet & Ellie writing duo, and aren't afraid of edgier writing, you might enjoy reading BDSM themed books written by Jet, the DARKER SIDE of the Masters' Writing Team.

The DARKER SIDE

Jet Masters is the darker side of the Jet & Ellie writing duo!

Romantic Suspense

Changing Roles Series:

THIS SERIES MUST BE READ IN ORDER.

Command Me

Control Me

Collar Me

Embracing FATE

Seizing FATE

Accepting FATE

HOT READS

A STANDALONE NOVEL.

Down the Rabbit Hole

Light BDSM Romance
The Ties that Bind

EACH BOOK IN THIS SERIES CAN BE READ AS A STANDALONE AND IS ABOUT A DIFFERENT COUPLE WITH AN HEA.

Alexa

Penny

Michelle

Ivy

HOT READS

Becoming His Series

THIS SERIES MUST BE READ IN ORDER.

The Ballet

Learning to Breathe

Becoming His

Dark Captive Romance

A STANDALONE NOVEL.

She's MINE

About the Author

Ellie Masters is a USA Today Bestselling author and Amazon Top 15 Author who writes Angsty, Steamy, Heart-Stopping, Pulse-Pounding, Can't-Stop-Reading Romantic Suspense. In addition, she's a wife, military mom, doctor, and retired Colonel. She writes romantic suspense filled with all your sexy, swoon-worthy alpha men. Her writing will tug at your heartstrings and leave your heart racing.

Born in the South, raised under the Hawaiian sun, Ellie has traveled the globe while in service to her country. The love of her life, her amazing husband, is her number one fan and biggest supporter. And yes! He's read every word she's written.

She has lived all over the United States—east, west, north, south and central—but grew up under the Hawaiian sun. She's also been privileged to have lived overseas, experiencing other cultures and making lifelong friends. Now, Ellie is proud to call herself a Southern transplant, learning to say y'all and "bless her heart" with the best of them.

Ellie's favorite way to spend an evening is curled up on a couch, laptop in place, watching a fire, drinking a good wine, and bringing forth all the characters from her mind to the page and hopefully into the hearts of her readers.

FOR MORE INFORMATION
elliemasters.com

facebook.com/elliemastersromance

x.com/Ellie__Masters

instagram.com/ellie_masters

bookbub.com/authors/ellie-masters

goodreads.com/Ellie_Masters

Connect with Ellie Masters

Website:
elliemasters.com
Purchase Direct:
elliemasters.com/shopify
Amazon Author Page:
elliemasters.com/amazon
Facebook:
elliemasters.com/Facebook
Goodreads:
elliemasters.com/Goodreads
Bookbub:
elliemasters.com/Bookbub
Instagram:
elliemasters.com/Instagram

Final Thoughts

I hope you enjoyed this book as much as I enjoyed writing it. If you enjoyed reading this story, please consider leaving a review on Amazon and Goodreads, and please let other people know. A sentence is all it takes. Friend recommendations are the strongest catalyst for readers' purchase decisions! And I'd love to be able to continue bringing the characters and stories from My-Mind-to-the-Page.

Second, call or e-mail a friend and tell them about this book. If you really want them to read it, gift it to them. If you prefer digital friends, please use the "Recommend" feature of Goodreads to spread the word.

Or visit my blog https://elliemasters.com, where you can find out more about my writing process and personal life.

Come visit The EDGE: Dark Discussions where we'll have a chance to talk about my works, their creation, and maybe what the future has in store for my writing.

Facebook Reader Group: Ellz Bellz

Thank you so much for your support!

Love,

Ellie

Dedication

This book is dedicated to you, my reader. Thank you for spending a few hours of your time with me. I wouldn't be able to write without you to cheer me on. Your wonderful words, your support, and your willingness to join me on this journey is a gift beyond measure.

Whether this is the first book of mine you've read, or if you've been with me since the very beginning, thank you for believing in me as I bring these characters 'from my mind to the page and into your hearts.'

Love,
Ellie

THE END